AN UNFRIENDLY CONVERSATION

"Look Deweese," said Slocum. "I'm not trying to start a fight with you."

"It seems to me that you are trying to provoke me. I won't have it. If you persist on being an annoyance, I shall have to deal with you."

Slocum was getting tired of the man's manner. He managed to be polite and insulting at the same time. Besides, Slocum knew he'd aroused Deweese's suspicions; if he let him get back to Tudor and the others, John wouldn't stand a chance . . . even if he did finally think of a plan. No. John could see where all this was heading. It was time to lower the odds.

Without thinking about what he was doing, Slocum said, "Then we'll say good-bye." Reaching up with his left hand, he seemed to tug his hat brim lower and turn to his right and walk away. Suddenly John spun his hat at Deweese's face. At the same time he fell to his right, quickly pulling the Colt across his body, thumb pulling the hammer back, forefinger pressing the trigger. He snapped his arm out before him, concentrating an instant on his aim, and released the hammer . . .

JAKE LOGAN

SLOCUM AND THE MOUNTAIN SPIRIT

JOVE BOOKS, NEW YORK

SLOCUM AND THE MOUNTAIN SPIRIT

A Jove Book / published by arrangement with
the author

PRINTING HISTORY
Jove edition / July 2000

The Penguin Putnam Inc. World Wide Web site address is
http://www.penguinputnam.com

ISBN: 0-515-12871-6

A JOVE BOOK®
Jove Books are published by The Berkley Publishing Group,
a division of Penguin Putnam Inc.,
375 Hudson Street, New York, New York 10014.
JOVE and the "J" design
are trademarks belonging to Penguin Putnam Inc.

PRINTED IN THE UNITED STATES OF AMERICA

10 9 8 7 6 5 4 3 2 1

1

At least this would be easy, Slocum thought as he
rode into Muffresboro. Just pick up Ed Cahill,
bring him back to Golden, and collect his money.
Then he could go someplace and relax for a while.
Good thing it was so simple. John didn't think he
could face anything too complicated. It was a fact,
Slocum was as low as he'd ever been; he was tired
and worn, feeling his years instead of his oats.

He certainly wasn't as young as he used to be,
and he didn't feel young either. All the wandering
around, all the fighting and death seemed to add
years to a man's life. Slocum was surprised at himself; he thought he'd become hardened to death
back during the war. Quickly, he closed that door
in his mind—thinking about the war wasn't going
to make him feel any better.

As he rode along slowly, his mind went back to
Ed Cahill, the young farmer he was supposed to
bring in—just another poor plow jockey who
couldn't make the land work. Old Ed had tried to

1

help himself get by with a little cattle rustling. Sheriff Loren had said that Cahill had gone a little loco when his wife died last year. He'd started to drink, and got sloppy pretty quick after that; the bills and the chores had started to pile up. Well, Ed was going to pay for his mistakes, Slocum thought as he rolled and fired a cigarette. *All I have to worry about is bringing him in.* It was an easy way to make a few dollars.

Slocum was lucky he'd ridden into Golden when the sheriff, an old friend of his, had been pressured into bringing Cahill in.

"Look, John," Loren had said. "If it was up to me, I'd let the poor bastard go with a fine and the return of the beeves. I've got enough trouble around here with some real bad hardcases. Cahill just tried something stupid, and ran when he was recognized. He's no gunman, that's the truth." Loren leaned his muscular, blocky frame forward to launch a gob at the spittoon.

"Just his bad luck that the local ranchers are up in arms over all the cattle they've been losing lately. I've got to find me some *real* rustlers, or I'd go bring Ed in myself. Anyway, he has a farm over in Muffresboro. You just see my buddy, Bob Randle—he's the sheriff over there. I'll write you a letter you can show him."

Loren leaned over his desk. "There's three silver dollars in it for you, and more if you want to stick around to help with the hard work when you get back. What do you say?"

Slocum, slumped in the only other chair in the little office, had put up his hands. "I'll bring in

Cahill, but that's all I'm up for right now. Think I could use a little rest. Soon's as I get back, I'm gonna use the money to get a bottle and a sweet little girl. Then I'm for a little hunting up in the mountains."

With Loren's description of Cahill, Slocum wandered into Muffresboro two days later. Muffresboro, like Golden, moved slowly in clouds of dust. Even sound seemed to drag itself out, voices slurring thick in the midday heat. Riding up to the wooden sidewalk, Slocum dismounted, tied his horse to a rail, and allowed himself a bellowing yawn and a stretch. Bob Randle, on feet as small as a Chinaman's, walked out of his office with a precise measured pace.

Just as John finished stretching and cracking his stiff joints, the scowling sheriff said, "Hell, do you want to wake the whole damn town?" He looked Slocum over suspiciously.

Fumbling in his pockets, Slocum answered, "Hold on a minute. I've got it right here."

"Got what?" All that could be seen of the sheriff's face were two flashing black eyes and a nose, white against thick black hair, beard, and eyebrows.

Slocum took out Loren's crumpled letter and made a weak attempt to smooth it out. Failing at that, he just handed it over to the dark little man.

Randle took the letter, though he didn't open it right away. He took off his hat—Slocum noticed that it was large, tan and very new. Randle's hair was salted with enough gray to make him look very distinguished.

Cursing to himself, the sheriff bent and fiddled with the hat, taking time to fit it just so on the top of his head. Unfolding the letter finally, he began to read to himself, lips moving with his eyes, pronouncing some of the words out loud. It took a while. When he was finished, he looked right up into John's eyes. "So you're going to take in this here Cahill?"

"That's right, Sheriff. Matt said you'd give me a hand if I had any trouble."

"Says here you ain't gonna have any trouble. Says Cahill's just a farmer, not even armed. Says you're deputized to bring him in."

Slocum was beginning to get irritated. "Look, it says all that, Sheriff. Just tell me where I can find him and I'll get out of your hair."

Still suspicious, Randle said, "Well, this is Matt's hand, all right. I just got a bad feeling about you, is all."

"I don't like you much either. Let me do what I came here to do, and we won't have to spend much time together. Where can I find Cahill?"

"That's one of the funny things about this. He's been seen in town. He ain't tried to run off. Guess he just figures no one knows. He come into town a few days ago, matter of fact . . . didn't seem much like he was tryin' to hide anything. I didn't think much of it till just now. Anyway, he ain't been back in town that I know of. Probably still out at his old man's place. He lives there with his little boy."

"You sure it was him in town?"

"Well, damn, boy, you'd figure people round here would know him, don't you?"

Slocum looked away for a moment and said, "Just tell me how to get to Cahill's place."

Randle stared pointedly at Slocum's gun. "You ain't fixin' to try any target practice, are you? Seems like you've had a lot of experience. This farmer boy ain't no fighter."

Slocum sighed. Everywhere he went, there was suspicion and anger and violence. "Look, I just want to bring this poor fellow back to Golden— alive. I don't want to hurt him. I just want to make an honest dollar."

The sheriff waited a moment, then told Slocum where to find Cahill.

Riding out of town, Slocum patted his horse's neck. "This is gonna be easy. I just know it. We'll rest up after, you and me."

He rode on, passing fewer and fewer houses as he left the town behind. He passed orchards and fields and people, and moved into the wild prairie. In the clear, dry light, he could see a little cabin and outbuildings on a bare hillside off in the distance.

His mind wandered as time passed. He thought it was strange that the cabin came no closer as he rode on. He felt light wind pushing at his back, hurrying him along. Slocum began to get impatient; he wanted to get this over with.

After a ride that never seemed to end, Slocum came up the rising land toward the cabin.

Normally, John Slocum would have been a lot more careful. Today, he was too distracted to take the time, and too much in a rush to get his money and relax. Without even stopping to look around, he rode right up and called out, "Hello the house!" He waited a second, and called out again, "Anybody home?"

A muscular redhead waddled around from the back of the cabin, pulling up suspenders. "Yeah, I'm comin'."

Slocum watched him as he approached, thinking that he'd never seen anyone who looked more like a farmer than this honyocker. He looked pretty angry too. "Who're you?" he demanded.

Lord, please don't let this get ugly, Slocum prayed.

"You Cahill?"

"Yeah, I'm Cahill. I asked you once already, mister. Who're you?"

John looked him in the eye, knowing that he had to get control of this and talk Cahill into coming in peacefully. For the first time, he realized that it was going to take some doing. Why didn't he think of this before? He'd wasted the whole trip daydreaming and feeling sorry for himself when he should have had his mind on his job. *I could get myself killed this way.*

Trying to improvise, he said, "Sheriff Loren sent me from Golden. He thinks you can help him identify some rustlers." A little white lie wouldn't hurt, might make things simpler. "He said something about a reward."

"I don't know nothin' about no rustlers." Cahill's voice got loud. "What're you talking about? Loren knows I stole them cows from that Johnson. . . ." Cahill made a sudden grab for the horse's reins.

Bucking the horse up quickly, Slocum drew his weapon, but Cahill lunged upward with surprising agility and pulled Slocum to the ground. They both ended up rolling in the dirt under the nervous mount's legs.

It happened so fast that neither had a chance to think. Slocum struggled against the man, realizing immediately that the farmer was far stronger. Slocum was hoping to roll on top and keep his gun, but the man was all over him. Kicking, yelling, and thrashing wildly, each man tried to get the upper hand.

When the gun went off, Slocum was looking directly into Cahill's wild eyes. They widened for just a moment, and then the bottom seemed to go out of them. John felt, for a brief second, like he was being pulled into deep, watery tunnels. . . .

Standing quickly, the heavyset farmer began to walk toward the cabin. Slocum pushed up onto one hand and one knee, breathing heavily. "Cahill!" he called. And again. "Cahill!" The farmer turned, and Slocum could see a widening circle of red on his chest. "Wait! Don't you see you've been shot?" Slocum got up and stumbled over to him, shouting, "Why the hell did you try that? I didn't want to hurt you, damn it!" Cahill stood, still as a statue, staring, while Slocum took dancing, nervous steps around him.

John could barely look at the man, who had

blood running down his pants now, his expression neutral and detached. Suddenly, Cahill seemed to notice that Slocum was there, wide-eyed and fidgeting, in front of him.

"I'm behind in my chores," he said, then turned and fell heavily to the earth.

John Slocum threw his hat to the ground and yelled, "Just my goddamned luck! Why me?" He knew the man was dead, but checked the body anyway. He wondered nervously how he was going to explain this to Randle. Now he was going to have to find a horse, bring the body back to town, and face all the crap that was surely going to come at him.

Slocum picked up his hat and thought awhile about just moving on, not returning to Golden. He'd have a good head start, but he knew that he'd be accused, probably, of murder. Besides, he wouldn't get his money, and he'd never be able to square himself with Loren. He sat back in the thin grass, bareheaded, the sound of wind and birds and buzzing flies all around. Slocum shook his head; already the flies and insects were at the body.

Suddenly, the silence was broken by a shout. "Pa!" Slocum turned quickly, and was hit by a small body. Fists and boots hit him from every direction. Little teeth bit his shoulder, drawing a cry of pain. Reflexively, he pushed the small body away, and a little boy flew across the ground, landing in a tangle. Slowly, the boy came to his feet, his face streaked with tears, blood running freely from a cut lip.

Slocum scrambled to his feet and backed away.

"Sorry, kid. I didn't mean to push you that hard. You surprised me."

Ignoring him, the boy ran to Cahill's body. "You killed my father! Why did you have to kill him?"

Slocum stared openmouthed at the child kneeling over the body. *Jesus, God, what have I done?*

The boy began crying in earnest. As he sobbed, calling his father over and over, an older version of Ed Cahill huffed around the corner of the cabin. "Oh, no!" he shouted. Out of breath and shaking, he began to curse Slocum. "Goddamn killer. Stinking bounty-hunting son of a bitch! You had to kill him, did you? Thought it was easier to take him back over a horse than on it, you bastard. He was just a farmer, not a murderin' fuck like you—"

Wait a goddamn minute, mister!" Slocum yelled. The old man stopped abruptly, put his head down, and started in to cry just as deeply as the boy.

Again Slocum was shocked into silence. *What have I done? What have I done?*

Quietly now, Slocum tried to calm Ed Cahill's two mourners. "He jumped me. I didn't have any choice. You must have seen it." He put his hands out, and took an awkward step forward. "I didn't want to hurt him. I just wanted to bring him back to town. He jumped me and tried to take my gun. I had to defend myself."

The old man pulled the boy behind him. They were a pathetic sight. Their faces were wet from crying; there was blood all over the lower part of the boy's face. "Go ahead and kill us too," the old man said.

John Slocum was in a turmoil. He wanted them

to understand but he knew they couldn't, ever. Slocum wasn't sure *he* understood. Death was something he was used to; killing other people was something that happened. Slocum knew he should have been more careful. He should never have let Cahill jump him like that. It was just damned sloppiness. *What's wrong with me? Maybe I did want it this way. Maybe I'm too used to killing anyone who gets in my way.*

"Go ahead, God curse you to hell. Don't leave any witnesses." The old man straightened up and looked into Slocum's eyes. "Do it, you animal bastard. We ain't scared of the other side." The old man's shaking hand pointed at Slocum. "*You* better be scared. You're bein' judged right now."

Slocum turned toward his horse; he felt his heart growing cold and shrinking. "I know you ain't gonna listen to me, but I didn't mean to kill him. And I'm not going to hurt either of you." He stopped and looked down at the ground. Slocum hadn't done much crying for quite a while, but he felt close to shedding tears now.

The three stood like that for what seemed to be a very long time to Slocum. The powerful sun beat down on them like a hammer; the wind blew; insects darted from tree to flower to Cahill's body and back again.

Finally, John looked up. He turned to the old man, still holding the young boy behind him, and said, "I'll need a horse to bring him into town. You can follow and make any arrangements—" He stopped when he saw their expressions. "I . . . I'll try to make them if you want—" The boy started

to say, "Daddy, Daddy," over and over. His grand-
father held him closer. Old Cahill started to say
something, then pointed behind the cabin.

Slocum dragged his feet walking to the little
lean-to behind the house. He picked out a horse
that seemed sturdy and led it out to Cahill's body.
Though the smell of the dead spooked the animal
somewhat, Slocum managed to get it quieted down
and standing still. He tried several times to lift the
inert form and heave it over the horse's back. It
didn't work. He began to sweat; his heart began to
pound so that he could hear it. He felt the two pairs
of horrified eyes on his back, and they drew out
any of the strength that he had left. His hat kept
slipping off; his feet slipped in the blood pooling
on the ground; the horse kept shying away.

John remembered seeing a tarp out back in the
cluttered lean-to. As he walked behind the house
again, he thought about how it could use some re-
pair, and wondered who would help the old man
keep the place together. The boy was too young to
be much help. Who would look after the boy? Who
would be there for him through the grief and despair and anger?

As he dragged the tarp around the house and
began wrapping Cahill's body, Slocum imagined
the boy thinking of revenge and hunting his father's killer through the countryside. There could
be a day, Slocum thought, when he'd turn to see
Ed Cahill's son aiming a pistol at his head. He'd
laugh and pull the trigger, and no one would mourn
John Slocum.

After much pulling and straining, with the two

still watching in angry, horrified silence, Slocum got the body over the horse. Before he rode off, Slocum looked at them, trying to think of something to say. He wanted them to know that it was all a mistake—an accident—that it wasn't his fault, that he wished he could undo all of it. He wanted them to know how sorry he was, and that he would never be able to forget. There was so much whirling around his head and heart that he was unable to get it to stop long enough so it could come out of his mouth. He was afraid he'd say the wrong damned thing and make it all worse.

Before he could get control of himself, the little boy looked right at him and said, "You killed my daddy."

Slocum, filled with empty pain, looked down at the ground. "Look," he said, "I'll send word through the sheriff. I—"

"Just get outta here, mister," Cahill's father said. "Just leave us alone." With his arm around the dazed boy, he turned to leave, then turned back. He looked at Slocum again and said, "I feel sorry for you. There won't be anyplace for you to hide from your sins."

John Slocum turned his big horse, and rode off feeling damned.

All the way back to town, Slocum thought about what the old man had said. It was true, he realized: all the killing, and all the pain he'd brought to so many families. . . .

At least he understood why Cahill had put up such a fight—he was protecting his son and his father. It seemed a true and honorable thing to fight for—to die for even. Slocum remembered feeling that way for a time in the war . . . in the beginning anyway. Later on was a different matter. Later on, fighting and killing was something that was going on everywhere around you, and there was no way to escape it; you did your best to make sure that when you did the fighting, someone else did the dying. Slocum thought of the war like a flood—when you got caught up in it, you did everything you could to keep your head above water and let it take you where it would. Sometimes it took you to some strange and evil places in some strange and evil company. *Like Kansas.* Slocum stopped thinking about the war abruptly—he didn't like these memories much.

He arched his back and kneaded the tight muscles in his shoulders. Damn, he was sore; Cahill had given him more of a pounding than he'd realized. Time was, a scrape like that wouldn't have slowed him down at all. Now . . . well, now a lot of things were a lot different. He seemed tired all the time, and his legs ached and his back hurt like the devil, and there were too many things he didn't want to think about. It seemed like his mind was a house with too many rooms he was afraid to go into.

Ed Cahill was lucky. He had someone to mourn him and someone to fight for. Good clean dirt was on his hands. All I got on my hands is blood.

Slocum hardly noticed where he was going. Leading the horse with the body draped over its middle, he hardly noticed the passing of time. He amused himself by going over and over his many sins. He chuckled humorlessly when he realized that there was hardly a commandment that he hadn't broken.

As he got closer to town, he began passing more people, and began noticing the whispers and the pointing fingers. By the time he pulled up in front of Randle's office, he'd collected a little crowd, all wanting to know about the body slung over the horse. Slocum dreaded his meeting with the lawman; he knew Randle would be furious. For that matter, he was going to catch it from Loren too.

Randle's office was locked; he must have been making rounds before dinner. Slocum didn't want to have to wander around looking for him, dragging Cahill's dead body around behind him; he didn't want to wait here trying to ignore the crowd either. Slocum began to worry. *What if Randle had to leave town? What do I do with the body then? How the damn hell did I get myself into this mess?* He always seemed to be shooting at someone, or being shot at . . . and then having to explain the whole mess to some law-dog.

Slowly, he got off his horse and began rolling his head back and forth, trying to ease the sore muscles along his shoulders. His head was pounding and he wished he could just get this over and done with, get to a saloon, and get a hard drink. Turning stiffly to a balding man wearing an apron, he asked, "Where the hell is Randle?"

The storekeeper blinked twice and took a step back. "How the hell would I know? I got a store to run." There were murmurs from the crowd—which was beginning to sound mighty unfriendly to Slocum. *Maybe it's just me.*

Suddenly the crowd parted and a voice shouted, "What is this?" Randle stomped up in a fury. "Goddamn you! I knew this was gonna happen the minute I set eyes on you."

Slocum had spent a long, miserable couple of days; he felt like he'd just about had enough. "Dammit, Randle. This farmer went crazy. He nearly killed me. If he wanted to stay alive he shoulda come along peacefully."

"Don't give me that crap. You're a professional. You shoulda been able to take care of a dumb-ass farmer like Cahill . . . without having to kill him."

For a long moment, Slocum was quiet. In his head, he saw himself shooting Randle and as many of these curious damn townspeople as he could . . . he saw himself putting his fist through the sheriff's hairy face. . . . Slocum felt his anger rising quickly, like a swirling red mist . . . moving up from his balls . . . when it reached his head, he'd fucking explode. . . .

Slocum quickly got hold of himself. Jesus, Lord! Was he crazy? The smart thing was to let the sheriff deal with burying Ed Cahill and taking care of the father and the son. Apparently, he didn't know about them yet. If he did, John realized, it would be real hard to get out of this town without some kind of trial, or hearing, or even a lynching. Slocum wasn't of a mind to give Bob Randle, or the good people of Muffresboro, any more reason to hate him. His best move was to get out of town, head back to Golden, get his money, and get lost.

"I'm sorry you feel that way, Randle. Cahill resisted arrest—plain and simple. He attacked a duly appointed deputy—me. He should have known better. I'm going to have to report this to Loren." Leaving Randle scowling, and the crowd buzzing, Slocum mounted his horse, turned, and rode off.

No one tried to stop him.

Two days later, Slocum returned to Golden. The hot, dusty air shimmered even though it was early morning, and sweat poured down his face, under his collar. He rode straight for Loren's office, his teeth clenched and his lips pressed together. Few gave him a second glance; he was just another exhausted rider moving through the swirling dust. Dismounting, Slocum arched his back, sore from the long ride and the nights without sleep. His eyes, red-rimmed, had heavy pouches beneath them. He'd spent both nights staring into the fire. He couldn't get the fight with Cahill out of his mind. He couldn't forget the faces of Cahill's son and Cahill's father. He was like a drowning man, Slocum thought, like a drowning man whose life passes before his eyes. He found he wasn't proud of his life and he wasn't proud of what he'd let his life become. John Slocum realized that he was just another drifter in a country filled with aimless wanderers. He'd done little that he could be proud of, little of any lasting worth. He cared for no one really, and no one cared for him. His only talent was killing other people. It used to be that he could take some pride in that . . . it didn't seem worth that much anymore.

He put his head up, straightened his shoulders, and walked into Matt Loren's office. The sheriff looked up at him and quickly stood. "Lord A'mighty, John. What happened to you? You look like hell."

Slumping into a rickety chair, Slocum told him about Cahill. From time to time, the sheriff frowned and said, "Damn," but let him go on. When he was done, Matt didn't look angry at all; he looked sad. "What's wrong with you, boy? You're better'n that. You got to admit, you didn't handle that too well."

Slocum took off his hat and ran a dirty hand through hair stiff with sweat. "I know. I know. I just been so tired lately; so damn tired. I just don't know what to do." Slocum looked out the window. "I don't know what's wrong with me."

The sheriff leaned his chair back onto its two rear legs. "I've seen this happen to men—especially lawmen who've been working tough towns too long. A man can get all worn out. Maybe it's time for you to settle down." Loren looked at him with kindly eyes, and said softly, "Maybe it's time to stop the drinking, start going to church, and start looking for a good woman."

Slocum rolled his eyes in disgust. "Not you, Loren. You telling me I should become a damned farmer?"

"You sure as hell don't sound happy now. You're going to have to do something."

Slocum stood and walked quickly to the door,

his spurs tinkling as his boots echoed on the wooden floor. "I guess I'll have to think about it."

"John, wait a minute." Loren stood and walked over. Reaching into his pocket, he said, "Here's your money." He counted out three dollars.

Slocum looked down at the money in his palm. He looked up at Loren and said, "Thanks a lot."

2

Slocum had started down the street toward the nearest saloon when he realized that it was Sunday morning. Nothing would be open until later in the day. He stood in the glare of the sun and wondered what he was going to do. He heard church bells ringing, shook his head, and began to laugh. "I must be crazy to think of walking into a church," he said to himself. "But that sure sounds like an invitation."

Slocum turned toward the sound of the bells and began to walk, thinking that he'd just sit and watch from the back where no one would notice him and . . . it'd be a nice quiet place to sit until the bars opened up.

When he reached the steps, he hesitated. Maybe he should just get a cheap hotel room, try and get some sleep. He changed his mind when he heard the ragged singing of a choir—they sang with little talent, but great spirit. Somehow that made the church seem friendlier, and he walked up to the door. He reached out, turned the knob, and pushed the door open.

Stepping in, Slocum turned to close the door and remembered his hat. Quickly, he grabbed it off his head, closed the door, and slowly turned. The First Calvary wasn't a large church. It held, Slocum thought, maybe fifty people. The interior was stark and white and neat as a pin. Huge doors were opened at the back and at both sides, letting in the blinding sun and allowing a breeze to move through the room. The ceiling was two stories high, and Slocum glimpsed beams and rafters, chandeliers and shadows, forming dizzying patterns above his head.

At the other end of the building from where he stood, the preacher, flanked by a small choir, sang lustily. Behind the pastor, the sun streamed through large double doors.

The First Calvary Church seemed a good place; a good place to talk to the Almighty. Slocum liked it . . . it reminded him of the churches he'd known as a boy back in Georgia.

It seemed that those days were centuries ago. John could barely believe that he was once the little boy he saw in his mind's eye—a little boy dwarfed by stern, powerful adults. He was an adult now himself . . . he didn't feel very powerful.

Slocum looked down the line of benches, beginning to notice the people filling most of the pews. Most of them seemed to have noticed him too. Trying desperately to get to an empty place quietly, he couldn't quite keep his spurs from jangling noisily. No matter how gingerly he walked—and mustn't

he have been a sight prancing like a stage villain—
his spurs betrayed every step. By the time he got
to a seat in the last row, everybody had glanced
back at him, including the preacher. The choir,
which had faltered a moment, continued and finished their hymn.

Trying to avoid the preacher's stare, Slocum
studied the people around him. The members of
the First Calvary—men, women, and children—
seemed to be a well-scrubbed group. Their clothes
were neat, their hair was combed, and their faces
were clean. John began to feel self-conscious about
his own slovenly appearance.

Everybody seemed to belong to a family or a
group; he was the only one sitting alone. *Wonder
what it'd be like to have a family?* To have companionship and affection and accomplishments—
that would be something. Maybe he *should* find a
nice girl and start a family; run a few horses
maybe. Instead of drinking up the three dollars . . .

Suddenly Slocum realized how quiet the church
had gotten. He sat up, looked around quickly, and
saw the pastor looking his way. Everyone else was
whispering or looking at him too.

John looked back over each shoulder; there
wasn't anyone behind him. *Jesus! They're looking
at me.* He put his head down, hoping to just sit
quietly until it passed. . . .

It was still quiet.

Looking up again, Slocum began to wonder if
the whole bunch was going to stare at him all day.
The sunlight still lit everything clearly, but it didn't
seem too damn friendly anymore.

The situation became more uncomfortable as the minutes passed. He held his hat by the edge and moved his fingers around the brim nervously. He shuffled his feet. He realized what he must look like in his dusty trail gear, battered boots. Dear God! He was still wearing his guns . . . he was wearing guns in church . . . on Sunday.

The service wasn't going to continue, not until he left. Silently, he prayed, Dear Lord, please let them go on with the service. I promise I won't bother you again.

Too embarrassed to stay, more embarrassed to move, Slocum began to sweat heavily. When the preacher turned, walked to a plain chair, and sat down, John realized he was going to have to leave or face a long standoff with the whole congregation of the First Calvary Church.

Finally, after many more agonizing minutes passed, Slocum stood.

He hesitated a moment. He wanted these people to understand that he meant them no harm. He wanted to say that he needed some peace and certainty in his life . . . he wanted to ask for their help.

Slocum knew he wasn't going to be able to say anything. Besides, why would these good people listen to a man who wore his guns to Sunday meeting?

Probably think I came to break up the service. Probably think I'm drunk.

Slocum began to work up a little anger; it felt good.

It wouldn't have hurt them to let him listen to the service . . . he wasn't bothering anyone. His face hardened as he slowly looked around at the faces in the church. He wished he could say something to wipe away the superior, disapproving looks on their faces. But then, how could he ever explain Ed Cahill to them?

Slocum walked out through the doors into the street, looking for a place where he could spend three dollars on strong drink.

3

There were more people on the street, it seemed, and the dust was thick in the air. In the church, the light had seemed clear and strong; here it was hazy.

The first two saloons Slocum tried, the Long-branch and the Palace, were closed up tight. The third, which had a sign that simply read "Noonan's" over the door, was open.

Looking into the dim interior, Slocum stopped a moment. There were no windows in the small room. Though there were quite a few chandeliers, none of them were lit. The only light came from the open doors to the street.

The room was decorated with tables, chairs, and scores of paintings of reclining nude women. Slocum wondered why there were so many—each one looked pretty much like the others. The bar wasn't long—rather short actually—but high shelves behind held an enormous number of bottles, cups, and glasses.

Three cowboys, dressed in dusty trail gear, had

their battered hats on the table in front of them. None even glanced at Slocum as he walked down the bar. They seemed too involved in their conversation. Whatever it was that they were discussing must have been important. Slocum could see that they were totally concentrated on the business at hand. They didn't seem angry—just serious.

Most of the tables in Noonan's still had chairs upended on them, and the unsmiling bartender had rows and rows of glasses in front of him. He would pick one up, wipe it once or twice inside and out, put it on one of the shelves behind, and pick up another. Slocum watched the tall, thin man mechanically choose, wipe, and place a number of glasses before he walked over and ordered a whiskey.

The dour bartender didn't miss a step. He looked up and said, in a clipped Scot's accent, "There'll be no liquor till after twelve noon. Can only serve'e Arbuckle till then."

John tried being diplomatic. "One drink is all I want. That'll hold me till noon."

"Won't do it. Again' the law."

Slocum sighed and pushed his hat back on his head. "I guess coffee'll have to do. Make it hot and real sweet."

While the bartender got the coffee ready, Slocum saw two women at the end of the bar. His eyes, accustomed to the dimness, made out that one was an older woman, dressed in a tight black dress. Her makeup was heavy and she seemed tired, or bored—or both. *Still, she does have an interesting body.* But it was her friend that caught his eye.

She walked right up to him, hips swinging and sassy. This one was young, plump, and ripe like a piece of fresh fruit. She wore a yellow dress, cut low in the bosom, hiked to the knee on one side. Her hair was light brown and long. You could strike a match on her sharp blue eyes.

"Hello," she said, like she really was interested. "Maybe I can help you."

Slocum's mood seemed to lighten. "Well, now, I don't doubt that you could." Slocum smiled.

She smiled right back, shifting from side to side. "I mean with a drink. I have a bottle in my room— ain't no law against drinking in your own place."

Slocum was beginning to feel good for the first time in what seemed like years. "That's a fine idea, Miss . . . ?"

"Moira. Name's Moira."

"Miss Moira. That's a pretty name. Yeah. Let's have a few drinks—maybe we could get to know each other better." Slocum put a hand on her hip.

She turned and started walking to the back, and Slocum fell in step beside her. "Now, let's get this settled," she said, businesslike. "I got rent to pay. . . ."

"Laddie," the bartender called. "Laddie! Your coffee."

Slocum didn't even hear him, and the three cowboys never even looked up.

The bartender went back to his job on the glasses, scowling at the perfectly good cup of coffee going to waste in front of him. He would be damned if he was going to throw it away.

• • •

The curtains were drawn, her room was dark. The bottle was half-empty. Slocum and Moira lay naked on the bed.

Slocum kissed her long and deep. He was sure now that he'd be able to work the tenseness out of his mood. His tongue explored her mouth, and she tried to suck his tongue into hers. His fingers grasped a breast, kneading hard.

Moira ran her hands down John's chest to his groin. She held him, then let go—and kept doing that over and over. She moaned as he began to lightly bite one nipple until it stiffened, then tried to take her whole full breast in his mouth. Slocum's neck began to ache, and he tried to shift position and work on the other breast and nipple. It helped for a while.

His cock stiffened a little and Moira began to cry out. He forgot about his neck, and resumed biting her nipples. He felt desire rising full in his chest, felt the heat in his head.

He shifted position so he could slide his fingers down her stomach, but it hurt his back, so he shifted again. As he did that, Slocum moved a finger between her legs and into her, trying to get her wet. Moira began to moan, "Oh, John," over and over, and Slocum became fully aroused as her hand continued to squeeze and release him.

He was having a hard time trying to find a comfortable position, but tried to concentrate on moving his finger in and out of her. That seemed to work, and he kept it up while kissing and licking her breasts and neck. *Thank God. All I needed was a pretty girl.* After the past few days, this felt good;

the liquor had softened the edges and now he was starting to feel relaxed. He knew he wouldn't ever do anything as stupid as going to church again—not if he had to give up playing with the likes of Moira. He was glad Matt didn't try to hold back any of the money . . . he wished there was something he could do for Cahill's little boy. . . .

Suddenly, he felt Moira move. She slid her tongue from his ear, down his neck, and across each nipple. He closed his eyes, laid back, and shifted his hips when jolted by a little pain. Moira groaned as her tongue moved down his stomach. His hands went into her hair and he pushed her head down onto his crotch.

"Okay, okay," she said quickly, and took him into her mouth, sucking until he was straight and hard. Her hand continued to squeeze and let go.

Slocum's desire was growing; he wanted to penetrate her and feel her move under him as he pushed in and out of her body. He didn't want to wait any longer to crush Moira under him. He pulled out of her mouth and moved down until he was lying between her legs.

He tried to thrust into her, but slid up; he grunted at the pain in his lower back. He tried again from a different angle, but missed again.

Moira, breathing hard, said, "Take it easy, cowboy. Don't be so anxious." Her hand came down between them and grabbed him in a firm, businesslike manner, and she began massaging her clit with the head of his prick. "Let me help."

Slocum's neck and shoulders began to ache sharply as he continued to move against her while still unable to get in. His movements became frantic as he met with no success.

"Wait! Wait, I said. Let me do it," the young girl gasped impatiently. "Slow down." She tried slipping the head into her, but it either moved up or slid to the side. Slocum's heavy body moved from side to side trying to aid her movements. His lust and need seemed curiously separated from his groin, and he started to go limp in her hand.

"Oh, hell." Moira let go of him and got out from under his body. She brought a hand up to his cheek. "Happens to the best of them, honey."

"Let's try again," Slocum said grimly. "I can do it."

Moira looked at him and sighed. "Sure you can. It's your money."

Half an hour later, the young whore moved from on top of John and sat with her back to the head of the bed. Reaching over to a table, she took a thin, black cigar and lit it. She took a deep drag and exhaled and patted Slocum's thigh. John lay next to her with his arm over his eyes. "Sorry," he said. "That never happened to me before . . . must be tired."

"Sure. You look beat. You'll be fine . . . but I have to get back to work. You have to get dressed—unless you have some more money to spend?"

Slocum sat up and began to pull on his clothes without replying. He wouldn't look at her. She shrugged and began to dress in silence.

John was lost in thought. He felt ashamed somehow. He knew this happened to lots of men once in a while. It didn't mean he wouldn't ever be able to please a woman again. Slocum pulled at a boot. He just felt so . . . so stupid—pawing at a woman and getting nowhere. *What's wrong with me?*

Moira, meanwhile, had finished dressing, and was at the door, tapping one little foot. "Mister? Can you hurry up? I have to get back." She opened the door, waiting.

Slocum didn't want to go out to the bar; he was sure that the bartender and the three cowboys would know what had happened just by looking at him. He knew that little bitch Moira would tell the older whore as soon as she left the room.

Is there another way out? "Moira," he whispered, "look, I feel a little funny about this . . . uh . . . could you—"

"You ain't gonna ask for your money back, are you?" she said in a loud voice. "Because, if you are. . . ."

Slocum held up both hands, "No, no. Nothing like that. Quiet down, would you? I just. . . . Oh, the hell with it." He stomped past her, spurs jangling. He saw the bartender look up from his work to stare. The three cowboys stopped in mid-discussion, glanced up at him, then resumed their talk.

The older girl sat perched on a bar stool, smirking. Slocum tugged down the brim of his hat, looked straight ahead, and made for the door. He felt like a fool.

The bartender watched Slocum as he sailed by,

and said, "Your coffee, laddie. You ain't goin' to waste this coffee, are ye?"

John could swear he heard a woman laughing as he walked out.

A few doors away, one of the saloons that were closed earlier had opened for business. John didn't notice the name. He walked up to the bar, which wasn't too crowded yet, and began to drink seriously. He hardly talked to, or noticed, the men around him. The bar began to fill up as Sunday passed.

Slocum's mind seemed to run in circles. It ran from his failure with Moira, backed through his humiliation at the First Calvary, the killing of Ed Cahill, and ended with worrying about the mess he'd made of his life . . . and started all over again. He lost count of the drinks and the time. He was more than a little drunk, and feeling more than a little sorry for himself, when he was startled by a gravelly voice.

"Must be a hell of a fix you're in."

Slocum looked up into the round, creased face of the bartender. The broad-shouldered little man had a kindly smile, and a thick head of wavy white hair. He was leaning on his elbows right in front of Slocum, his teeth glinting in the candlelight. John thought hazily that it must be night.

"You talkin' to me, bartender?"

My name's Gerry. I've been watching you put away one drink after another through the afternoon. You've barely said a word to anyone—why, you've hardly moved. I can almost hear you thinkin' and you haven't smiled once. It must be a heavy load you're carrying. Here, have one on me." Gerry reached over to pour Slocum a drink. John tried to read the label, but couldn't focus his eyes.

As the bottle returned to the shelf, two men down at the other end of the bar began to argue. Both were tall and hard-bitten. Though neither raised his voice, they were clearly menacing. Conversation around the two quieted, then ceased.

Gerry looked at Slocum sadly. "Why can't people discuss their problems reasonably?" He straightened, sighed, and walked down the bar. John noticed, for the first time, the size of Gerry's hands and biceps. By the time Gerry reached the two men, the crowd had backed away, sensing trouble. From behind the bar, Gerry tried to be diplomatic. "Gentlemen, let me buy you both a drink and then we can—"

Slocum was having trouble getting the room to stay still, but it looked like both men, ignoring the bartender's efforts, had started to brush back their dusters and go for the guns at their side. In a blur, Gerry vaulted over the bar and was between them. Knocking both guns up with either hand, the powerful little man brought his fists down hard onto the faces of the men on either side of him. Blood sprayed from two noses, and both men dropped awkwardly to the floor. When both made a move to get up and continue the fight, Gerry looked down at one and then the other and said quietly, "How stupid are you gentlemen?"

Their faces painted with blood, their eyes already blackening, both leaned back and looked away, the fight gone out of them. The crowd began talking excitedly. "Nice goin', Gerry," someone called out. "How in hell does he do that?" someone else asked. Gerry bent, grasped each of the would-be fighters by the upper arm, and grunted as he brought them to a standing position. Slocum smiled. *How in hell does he do that?*

Everyone went back to their drinks, talking in loud voices. Gerry led both men by the elbow to an empty table, and began what looked like a lecture, right forefinger moving like a baton. He never threatened or raised his voice. Slocum couldn't overhear what was said. Somehow, though, before returning behind the bar, Gerry got them both to shake hands.

When Gerry was back in front of him, Slocum grunted, "Well, shit, I thought you were going to get them two to kiss and make up."

Gerry just smiled, and looked embarrassed. "Oh, now . . ." he mumbled. "I just hate to see anyone hurt or in trouble."

"Everybody's in trouble," Slocum said.

"Well, that's right. But some are in more trouble than others, and sometimes a kind word or some advice can help. Sometimes, gettin' drunk's the best thing you can do . . . like in your case."

Even though Slocum was having a hard time keeping his head still, and could only make out wavering forms, he tried to fix the man with a hard stare. "What do you know about my case, friend?"

"Nothing really," Gerry said calmly. "Anyone can see you're going over something deep, and you look all stiff and tensed up. When something's got you in its teeth like that, you need to back off it, look at it from a different angle." He laughed. "Drinking too much'll sure make everything look different."

John relaxed and smiled. "Yeah, I guess that's true enough."

"Of course it is . . . for now. You can't fix your troubles if you stay drunk too long, though. My dear father used to tell me, when I was just a lad, 'Watch a man, Gerard,' he said to me. 'Watch a man when he's in trouble, and you can tell what kind of man he is.' "

Slocum, slumped over the bar, began to think. Gerry stood in front of him, leaning on his hands, watching; Slocum thought he'd never seen anyone but an Indian hold himself so still for so long.

John Slocum finally stirred and looked up. "You don't understand. I've . . . I've *wasted* my life." His speech was slurred, and he had trouble keeping his head up. "I've stolen and killed . . . hell, I've probably broken every commandment there is. But it's all for nothing. I've broken things . . . I just never *made* anything. I can't explain it." Slocum reached for his glass, missed, and got it on the second try.

The bartender, in his gruff way, looked sympathetic. "Maybe you should try Mother Church," he said. "Many men have found peace there."

"Nah." Slocum roused himself. "Fuck those hypocrites. I tried that—bastards. . . ." It was too much trouble to find the words. Easier, he thought, to drink—especially since the drink was right there in his hands.

Gerry was gone. Slocum painfully turned his

head from side to side looking for him. It was hard to focus. He finally saw him talking to several other men. Gerry seemed to move all over the large room, talking and laughing, serving drinks and cleaning up. Slocum, despite his difficulties following the busy man, enjoyed watching him work. It was amazing to see a man so capable and so confident. Everyone seemed to like and respect the powerful little bartender. Slocum wondered what it would be like to be admired like that; to be useful.

I sure don't feel very useful. Only used up and full of hate. *And drunk; better not forget drunk.* Being drunk didn't make him feel very much better about himself. Shoulders and back and knees didn't hurt as much, though, that sure was something. They'd been giving him the devil lately. Right now, they didn't even feel like they were there. *In fact, seems like my whole damn body don't feel like it's there.*

Slocum was no stranger to drinking—he'd spent a good deal of his life drinking too much. Usually, however, drinking made him expansive, or reckless, or horny, or mean, as well as numb. Now, he felt empty and sorry for himself. He thought about Cahill's boy and decided to think about something else. All he could think about were the many problems in his life. Maybe he should try to think about other people some of the time; maybe he was too selfish. *That's my problem—always thinkin' about my damn self.*

Slocum finished his drink. As he put the glass down, he began to watch the residue in the shot glass slowly spread back down the sides. Patiently, oblivious to everything else around him, Slocum waited for all of the liquid to return to the bottom. Throwing his head back—and almost pitching himself off the stool—he tried to empty the glass totally. But he could still see a tiny bit there, sliding back. . . . Maybe he should get another drink. *Couldn't hurt.*

Looking up, he was surprised to see Gerry in front of him again. *Forgot about him.* "Looks like you need another," Gerry said. Pouring, he asked, "Solve anything yet?"

By this time, Slocum could only shake his head; speaking was too goddamn difficult. He felt tired. Getting up off the stool, he took the full glass from his new friend—*damn good man, that Gerry*—and downed it in one gulp. He felt the drink sliding into his body and slowly seeping down into the deepest part of him. The room began to swim faster and faster until the light was gone.

In the dark, Slocum's body shot up and he tumbled and whirled in every direction, at once swallowed by the brown sky with the roar of flood waters in his ears. The preacher from First Calvary Church was shouting in his face, but Slocum couldn't hear a thing. At the preacher's feet, Moira lay naked, her legs spread, wet pubic hair shining the only light he could see. Two fingers of one of her hands were between her legs holding brownish lips apart, while the middle finger of the other hand slowly moved up and down.

Spinning, whirling past them, Slocum bounced through flames into the streets of a town lit by flickering torches smoking and the flare of rifles and pistols. Screaming shadowed riders, running forms yelling for help, the cries of women and children, and curses became the sound of waters flowing, and he began to pick up speed until he was moving so fast that he felt his face distorted.

John Slocum felt himself pitch and whirl sickeningly. Suddenly his body slammed into another. Cahill's face filled his vision, distorted, screaming curses fading into the sounding waters of the sea.

Swinging facedown over a dusty floor, John felt a shout of anger and fear, of frustration and bile and desire, build up from the tops of his thighs filling his insides with a mighty yell. If he could release that scream of rage he could be free. He put everything he had into it, flinging every deep piece of the hated killer inside him away from his soul and memory. He pushed so hard that it all stuck in his throat, shutting off his breath, rumbled around his chest, and jammed back again into his throat. He felt his neck muscles balloon.

Suddenly, the roaring of the sea became his voice, and the faces and the memories and pieces of his brain and red heart gushed out of his mouth like the steaming smoke screaming from a train stack.

"Holy shit Jesus! Lookit that!" a voice said in his ear.

Concentrating every part of his body and mind, he tried to push out every bit of the self he hated, but it was like having a baby push clouds of steam. He sucked in air and spat again, trying to get out every last piece of the John Slocum nobody wanted. But there was a little bit left in the shot glass no matter what he did.

So he opened his eyes.

4

When he opened his eyes, everything was dripping sunlight; everything was distorted by a dazzling brightness that stung his eyes like needles. He was in an uncomfortable straw-filled bed and his head throbbed in an even booming tempo with such forceful pain that he almost cried out. He would have done anything to make it stop. He shut his eyes tightly, and even that hurt.

"Well, son, you're alive," shouted Gerry, smiling. His boiled white shirt was crisp and clean as new. Slocum tried to open his eyes again, but when he did, the pain spread from his head into his body—especially his stomach. He thought he was going to be sick. He hoped he was going to be sick.

He opened his eyes just a little. The light was unbearable. Slocum groaned miserably and turned his head—and he almost *was* sick then.

"You'll be fine and dandy before you know it."

Why the fuck is he yelling? John wondered. He tried to tell the bartender to please, dammit, whisper, but the sides of his throat were stuck together. Slowly, moving *very* slowly, Slocum turned to the water glass resting on a stool by the bed. The clicking of the straw bedding beneath him hurt his ears.

A hand gently touched his, stopping him from drinking. "No, no. That won't help yet. Try this first."

A glass was thrust into his hand. Slocum, finally managing to sit up, looked into it. The glass was filled with a thick, reddish liquid. It was hard to see what was floating around in it—but something sure was. Slocum didn't like the look of it—it looked like blood.

"Just close your eyes, and drink it down all at once. Don't take a breath, don't stop to taste it, or worry about what's in it. Just get it into you. Take my word—it never fails."

John squinted at his friend, too sick and too weary to argue. He shut his eyes and did as he was told.

As the contents of the glass went down his throat, Slocum got enough of a taste and enough of a whiff to make him realize that he was making a huge mistake. It tasted like blood mixed with kerosene and grass. He tried to stop drinking in mid-swallow, but Gerry's hand quickly came up and tipped the rest of the vile stuff down his throat.

When it hit his stomach—and Slocum could swear he heard it *plop* like a stone—his eyes popped open and his whole frame shuddered like a wet dog's.

"Goddamn you! What the hell did you poison me with?" Slocum bellowed. He could actually hear his stomach gurgling in revolt. He actually *felt* his bowels move—like he'd swallowed a snake. For a second, he thought he was going to vomit; then he felt like he was going to explode. What he did do was belch—long, loud, and strangely enough, very satisfyingly.

Slocum looked at the glass and then at Gerry.

Gerry smiled and said, "Well, it *did* give you back the power of speech." He chuckled with great good humor.

"What the hell was in that—gunpowder?"

"Oh, it's a secret recipe. Been in my family for generations." Gerry grinned. "A little tobacco, some medicinal herbs—that's the secret part— some vegetables, a little of the hair of the dog. . . . A little of this, a some of that. It's a secret, you see. But it *does* work, now doesn't it?"

"If you were meaning to kill me, maybe. Damn!" Slocum spat. "That stuff's terrible. I think it's worse than having the hangover." Slocum lay back down. He *did* feel a little bit better, but he sure as hell wasn't going to give that grinning fool any satisfaction. Strange, though. His head felt lousy, and his stomach was still moving, but he felt a lot less like dying. He groaned and belched again.

"Now. You just rest up awhile. You'll be wanting the convenience outside for the rest of the morning; and mind you, drink plenty of water. But you'll be cleaned out in no time at all. I guarantee it." Gerry laughed in good fellowship, and thumped John on the ankle, obviously pleased with his good work.

Slocum groaned, belched a third time, passed an evil wind, and scowled.

The bartender took a black stub of a cigar out of his shirt pocket and put it in his mouth. Seeing Slocum's terrified glance, he said, "Don't you worry. I won't smoke this while you're in such a delicate condition." He laughed again. "We'll wait for all the poison to be out of your system."

Poison! Slocum put a hand to his stomach. "Poison!"

"No, no, no. Not the cure." Gerry held up a hand to calm his patient. "No, the drink is the poison, son; the whiskey and spirits. Oh, it *is* divine stuff—given to us by the Good Lord to make life in this vale of tears tolerable ... to let us know, oh-so-briefly, how the angels feel. But it *is* a poison too. Oh, yes, it is. Too much—as you right well know—is harmful. And a lifetime dedicated to spirits is a calamity indeed."

Slocum felt a movement in his bowels and tried to ignore it.

Gerry went on. "Like many blessings in this world, the drink is also a curse."

Slocum felt pressure, strong pressure, and a sudden need to relieve himself—quickly. As he jumped and ran from the room—not caring that his pants were left on the floor by the bed—he heard Gerry's booming laughter. "Don't worry, boyo! The exercise will be good for you too!"

5

By midafternoon, John Slocum was exhausted. He'd lost count of the number of times he'd been to the foul-smelling privy out back. He felt weak and drained . . . and his ass burned something awful . . . but his head didn't ache so much, and he could see clearly again. He swore he'd never take strong spirits ever again. Or eat solid food.

After the first few trips, Gerry kept after him to drink glass after glass of water. "Can't let you dry up, can we? We've got to keep water in that tired old body of yours, or you'll really get sick."

Of course, the man was right . . . as usual. But as Slocum felt better physically, he began to have the time to remember. By Monday evening he was torturing himself again.

He just didn't know what to do. Drinking was out, that was manifest. He didn't dare try another woman. He was too damn beat to try to take out his frustrations fighting. Even Gerry's cheerful, philosophical company was beginning to wear thin.

If it came to *that*, his own company was wearing thin.

What could he do? He'd never felt like this—not ever. He was too exhausted to keep busy; too exhausted to keep himself from thinking about Cahill's son and father; too exhausted to forget Moira and his shame . . . Heaven help him, would he ever be able to bed a woman again? Life would be terrible without being able to find pleasure in a woman's arms. He sighed. There'd been so many—short, round, long, dark, tall, fair, shy, and ribald. It made him feel worse to think about what he'd never enjoy again.

It must be a sign of age, he thought. There's the first part of me to turn useless. First, his privates would only be good for taking a piss; his legs'd go next. He wondered if he dared look in the mirror—would he be surprised at the gray in his hair and the wrinkles on his face?

Slocum sighed again, and turned his head toward the window. He didn't need to look in any mirror. He knew what he'd see—a tired, mean old man who'd lost the ability to please a woman, or himself. Soon, he'd be sitting a rocker instead of a horse; whittling sticks, telling stories about the old days. . . .

Slocum snorted. Probably wouldn't live long enough to enjoy that much peace, he realized. With his reputation, some drunk kid with a borrowed gun would shoot him. Or someone he'd wronged would come gunning for him. He could see it now; one day he'd turn around, and there'd be Cahill's boy with a gun in his hand. "You bastard!" he'd yell.

"You killed my father in cold blood." There'd be a flash and a roar, and the smell of gunpowder, and he'd end his days rolling in the dust and horseshit in the street of some lousy little town, blood foaming from his mouth, trying to scream for his mother to make the pain go away . . . probably wouldn't be lucky enough to die . . . end up being a cripple . . . begging in the streets . . . serve him right . . .

Jesus! He was driving himself crazy.

He just didn't know how to stop.

It was dark when he woke. The stillness and quiet told him that it was late in the night or early in the morning. He swung his legs over and found he could stand without getting dizzy or sick. Thank the Lord for small favors, he thought.

Walking gingerly to the window, Slocum wondered, for the thousandth time, what he was going to do. He felt worse than he had before he got drunk. Every part of his body ached with a dull, deep pain; he was worried like he never was before—and he'd been in some tight places. He couldn't forget the things he'd done that he shouldn't have, and the things that he didn't do that he should have. He felt like every man's hand was raised against him.

Staring out into the still night and the sky full of stars like grains of sand, he sat and thought for a long time. He rolled and smoked one cigarette after another, enjoying none of them . . . it was just something to do to keep his body occupied while he tried to keep his mind on the problems that had to be solved.

Slocum realized, sometime during the long night, that he had to do *something*—he couldn't survive long this way. He thought of, and discarded, many ideas and notions—run to New York; run to San Francisco; run to Canada . . . He didn't have enough money . . . and he realized that he didn't have enough time. Settle down somewhere, get a job—but what could he do? Become a clerk? A farmer? Who would hire him? Where would he go? He couldn't stay where he was, and he couldn't imagine a place where he'd be safe from others or from himself.

He had to do something.

But what?

When dawn's rosy fingers spread over the eastern sky, John Slocum had made up his mind. He wasn't going to hide in a back room of this or any other town. He decided that, if he was indeed sick of everything, he was going to hole up somewhere and figure out what was wrong with his life. Maybe that was the answer—there was still enough wilderness to get lost in. Maybe he'd just get lost and stay lost.

While dressing, he suddenly remembered his horse and his gear. He'd left everything in the livery, but he'd only intended to get a little drunk and move on to . . . to . . . who knows where. Damn, he thought, as he quickly buckled his gun belt and searched the room, making sure he left nothing behind. As he looked under the bed, he thought, Just like me—no plans, no brains. Now I'll probably be without a horse.

Leaving the room, which was at the back of the saloon, he found Gerry already at work cleaning glasses. Slocum wondered how the man managed to always look so neat and clean; to always seem to be in control of a situation; to be so cool, so calm.

"Jesus and Mary—save us and preserve us," the bartender said. "Look at you. I'm glad to see that you're still living, but you look like hell."

"Thanks," said John. "I'm glad to see you too." He sat down at the bar.

As soon as Slocum's bottom touched the stool, Gerry was in front of him. "What'll you have?" he asked suspiciously, eyes narrowed.

Slocum smiled at him. He waited a moment, then said, "Arbuckle."

Gerry smiled back.

How does he keep them so clean and shiny?

Coffee, steaming hot, appeared before him in no time. Slocum picked it up and, blowing to cool it off, took a few quick sips.

Grimacing, he looked at Gerry in surprise. "This is terrible! Damn." He put the cup down and pushed it away. "Well, I'm glad I finally found something you *don't* do well. You make the worst coffee I ever tasted."

Gerry stood up straight and, unsmiling, looked at John squarely. "I didn't make it," he said in a quiet voice.

Both men stared at each other for several moments. Neither moved a muscle.

Suddenly, at the same instant, both broke out into wild laughter. Gerry held on to the bar, shaking; Slocum nearly fell off his stool, and actually had to hold on to his stomach. Gerry laughed so hard he began to cough uncontrollably in between barks of laughter. Both men had tears streaming down their faces.

After a while, the laughing tapered off into groans and moans; Slocum was surprised to find himself on the verge of real tears. He scared himself—he almost wasn't able to pull himself back. . . . He knew that if he started, he'd never be able to stop. After a moment, he looked at the solid bartender and said, "Thanks. I needed that. It felt damned good."

Gerry smiled his smile. "My pleasure."

When Slocum returned from the livery stable, he walked into the saloon and straight up to Gerry. "Seems I owe you the money you advanced the stable man the other night. I'm beholdin'. I probably wouldn't have a horse if it wasn't for you. Shit, I probably woulda killed myself with the hangover alone if it wasn't for you." He counted out a few coins into Gerry's hand. "The money don't pay all that I owe you either."

Gerry got busy around the bar. "I do what I do because I want to. You don't owe me anything."

Slocum touched Gerry's hand with his forefinger. "If you ever need anything—anything—get word to me. I mean that. Please."

After a pause, the man sighed and said, "I will do that." Smiling again, he asked, "And what will you do with yourself now?"

"Well, I don't rightly know. Yet. I thought I

might do some huntin' up in the mountains while I was trying to decide. I'll know by the time I come down. I'll stop by and let you know what I've decided must be done."

"I think that's wise, and I'll appreciate your stopping by to tell me."

Gerry picked up a glass and began to wipe it with a cloth. He stopped wiping for a moment and looked at Slocum seriously.

"Might I make a suggestion, John?"

"Of course. You ain't steered me wrong yet."

"Whatever you decide, you'll remember that you should think carefully? That sometimes the best things that you must do are the hardest? You'll remember that you want to do yourself some lasting good, eh?"

"I'll remember. And I won't forget all the good you've done for me either." Slocum looked away a moment. "One more thing."

"What is it?"

Slocum hesitated. How could he say this? "How do you do it? I mean, how do you stay so calm? You always seem to be in control of things . . . you do everything so well, and everyone listens to you. . . ." Slocum let it go; he just didn't have the words.

Gerry looked sad. "Oh, this is just an act, is all. I've got troubles as deep and as dark as any man's, sure enough. I just try to keep them from beating me down, and pushing me too far from the joy . . . the issue's often in doubt, let me tell you."

"Why don't you let *me* try to help *you*?"

"Funny thing," Gerry said, looking at the glass

in his hands. "I've always had trouble doing just that. Sometimes, it's true I do let them build up in me. . . ." He clasped his big paw onto Slocum's shoulder and smiled. "Maybe someday I'll take you up on that offer."

"I'd be glad to help—anytime you're ready, anyplace you want."

"Thank you. Now. You must be off, I see. Go on."

Slocum smiled and nodded. They looked at each other for a long moment. Then Slocum picked up his saddlebags and walked away. He looked back once—Gerry was wiping the bar busily and singing a song in a booming voice about a buxom girl named Sally.

6

John Slocum rode out of Golden thinking hard. He'd stocked up on basic supplies with his remaining money, gotten his horse out of the livery stable, and ridden away without a backward glance. He'd ridden into some desperate and dangerous situations in his life, but he realized that he was now as desperate as he'd ever been—the last few days had proved that to him.

He hardly noticed his surroundings and hardly gave conscious thought to his direction—though he knew, somewhere in his head, just where he was going. In the beginning of his long journey, his mind was stuck in a familiar rut, one that he recognized and was becoming almost comfortable falling into—Cahill, Cahill's boy, Cahill's father, First Calvary, Moira. . . . He wasn't sure when it began, but sometime during that ride he left those familiar guilts and his mind just began to wander. He never noticed anyone, never acknowledged anyone, never remembered seeing anyone. He barely recalled, in later years, the route he took.

The weather was mild, sunny, but he barely realized that. He saw only the years gone by—women he'd loved (or thought he'd loved), men he'd fought; hard riding, hard loving, hard fighting . . . a hard life. As always, however, he ended up thinking about Cahill's son. He thought about him and worried about what that young man's life would be like because of what he'd done to his daddy. He thought and worried until he tired himself out.

Lucy Doddwell was happy for any company. Even if it was her cousin, Thomas. It wasn't that she minded Thomas that much—though he had begun to puff himself up considerably since he'd begun working on that newspaper. No, it wasn't Thomas that got her goat. It was that little washed-out wife of his, Maria, with her superior manner. Lucy felt that if she had to sit through just one more lecture on how very civilized Cleveland was, and how very uncivilized Golden was . . . well, she would pour a whole pot of tea over that little bitch's head, that's all. She smiled at the thought.

Still, Lucy *was* glad for the company. Frank worked all day in the store, trying to get them ahead, and she knew that if they wanted to raise a family . . . well, she shouldn't complain; it just didn't do any good.

It was just that Maria—who *insisted* on pronouncing her name Ma-RI-a—"just like the French, don't you know"—acted as if she was doing them all a favor by her very presence. What did Thomas see in her?

"Lucy? Are you listening?"

"Oh, I'm sorry, Maria—"

"Ma-RI-a, Lucy, Ma-RI-a. Just like the French—"

"Yes, I know."

"I do wish you'd remember. I don't know how many times I've had to remind you—"

"We saw the most unusual man today, Lucy," said Thomas. "Didn't we, dear?" He'd quickly sensed that it was time to change the direction of the conversation. He couldn't understand why his cousin was so resentful of his wife. They could all benefit from her cultured upbringing and attitude.

"Yes, indeed, Thomas," said Maria, "Quite the frontier character. The countryside is full of this awful class of people; it positively abounds with them. It's a shame that nothing can be done about it, but in these primitive conditions . . . I was quite nervous, I must admit. We were riding along, quite peacefully, and we came upon this . . . brigand . . . armed to the teeth, like so many of these ruffians, muttering to himself. Who knows what someone like that is capable of—"

"Surely there are ruffians even in a proper town like Cleveland, Ma-RI-a," Lucy said.

"But Lucy, dear. In a real city—one could hardly call a metropolis like Cleveland a *town*—they have a real police force. Why, if I hadn't been with my husband, Lord knows what could have happened. A woman can't—"

"I must say, it *was* quite unusual," Thomas put

in. He began to nervously fuss with his clothes—
smoothing seams, picking lint. He always seemed
to be trying to keep Lucy and Maria—Ma-RI-a—
from escalating their conversations into arguments.
"Quite unusual. He was a rough-looking chap, to
be sure. Dirty clothes, filthy boots; we could smell
him before we could see him, believe me. And Ma-
RI-a is quite right, he was muttering to himself the
while, and running his hands over his pistol—a
very large pistol. Strange thing was, he never noticed us; not even for a moment. Didn't even try
to control his mount—why, when I looked back,
the animal was cropping grass by the side of the
road, and that madman was muttering and growling
and twitching."

"Really, Thomas, Ma-RI-a. Don't you think
you're both making too much of this?" Lucy hated
being put in the position of defending every tramp
rider in the territory. But these two acted as if there
should be trolley cars and symphony orchestras on
every street. "He doesn't seem to have threatened
either of you. Perhaps the poor man was in trouble.
The Christian thing to do would have been to try
and help the poor soul." There. That should quiet
their insufferable superiority; Thomas was becoming quite as bad as Ma-RI-a.

"Why, Lucy. Are you suggesting—"

Thomas intervened again. "No, Lucy. Really,
you had to have been there. His face was stamped
with every vice and brutality known to the sinful
race of man. The lout was capable of anything—
anything. I intend to write an editorial. . . ."

Lucy's mind began to wander. . . .

• • •

When the light began to fade, he came out of his deep, dark thoughts long enough to find a place to camp. He had no desire to eat and very little energy; his head still throbbed dully and his neck and back and shoulders and knees ached. He thought a moment about collecting wood, making a fire, and forcing a meal into his stomach, but collapsed instead into his roll after ground-tethering his horse. He realized that he was forgetting the habits he'd developed in a lifetime on a dangerous frontier— the habits that had become second nature and had saved his life many times. He didn't care. He was asleep the moment his head hit the saddle he'd set down as a pillow.

He awoke late to sunshine and birdsong. He tried to hold on to the memory of his dreams, but gave up as they faded back into the hidden places in his mind. The dream had seemed so real, so urgent, so important. It was something he should have remembered—but it was too much trouble to hold on to.

Slocum stretched and groaned, his muscles protesting. He considered trying to go back to sleep— he was so, so tired—but he realized that it was best to keep moving until he found the right place. He hoped he had enough brains to recognize the right place when he *did* find it.

He tried working out the kinks in his tired body, but it didn't seem to do much good. Getting old, getting slow, he thought. Might as well get used to it. Won't be good for the hard, fast life I've been living anymore. Should be thinking about the future instead of chewing over the past.

Resolving that he would spend more time trying to puzzle a way out of the scrape he'd gotten himself into cheered Slocum somewhat. He'd just have to bear down like he'd always done in the past and he'd figure something out . . . he always had. By the time he was ready to go, the sun was high. Though he was still pretty sore, and didn't want to think much about food, his spirits were beginning to lift.

Maybe all I need is a little rest and a little time off by myself. Relax a little, hunt a little, and I'll be as good as new in a few days. Been through some tough times . . . have to rest up a bit before I can get back to my old self. I'm just a little wore out is all.

Starting out and moving up into the hills, Slocum felt better than he had in months. He still hurt all over, and had some of that old hangover pain, but the world seemed a little brighter. As he moved on, swaying gently with his horse's motion, he noticed the sun beaming through the trees. He began to appreciate the mildness of the day and the dry crispness of the air. The bright green woods around him were full of life and rich with scent. Slocum found that he was beginning to wake up and enjoy the day for a change.

Watch a man when he's in trouble and you can tell what kind of man he is.

The wisdom of Gerry's father sat in his head. It was like a challenge that he didn't want to back away from; it was a call to action and a banner that he felt he could rally his forces around. Slocum began to feel confident.

Ten minutes later, the powerful sun pulsing into the forest reminded him of the hard light inside the First Calvary Church. He began to remember what other people saw when they looked at him, and the rising spirits of the early morning began to sink as the sun rose higher in the sky.

By evening's camp, he was up past the foothills and into the mountains . . . and deep in despair again. By evening's camp, he was trying to number the men he'd killed during his long life. Slocum thought to try to figure out how many innocent men he'd murdered, and how many he'd shot in self-defense. At first, he found it difficult to concentrate, but he found that the job became easier if he didn't let himself become distracted by the world around him. As time went by, he found it simple to let himself go, to fall back into his memory until the forest and hills all about disappeared.

In his mind, John saw muzzle flashes, heard the roar of pistols and rifles, the sound of knives ripping flesh . . . men screamed and cursed, women wailed, children cried. Sometime during that sleepless night, the cool night, he realized that he had to attack the problem with a system. How many men killed during the war? How many killed during the war while he was with the Army of Northern Virginia? How many killed in Kansas? How many killed just after the war? How many killed since he came West? *Cahill.*

Should he count those killed during the war?

They would be a powerful number . . . and most had to be considered innocent, didn't they? He knew nothing about the men he'd killed then; he'd had no way of judging them. But during a war a man was following orders; he was just part of a greater conflict over which he had no control. He'd believed then in what he was fighting for. The men he'd shot were innocent—but what would have happened to him if he'd refused to fight? What then? He was just one of a legion of men fighting and shooting. . . .

I shot most of them from ambush, he thought. A sniper sitting in a tree, waiting to see a blue patch and the gold braid of an officer amidst the forest's green; aiming so carefully, then gently squeezing the trigger. Off quickly to another place to hide and wait. It was a job. Thousands of us, shooting at thousands of others. How could a man count the killed or wounded? No, John Slocum decided. I can't be held accountable for the men I shot at during the war. We were all fighting . . . it was beyond anyone's control. I'm clear of those deaths. He felt relieved. The war wouldn't bother his conscience.

Except for Kansas.

Kansas wasn't a war—it was something else. The war was bad, but Kansas was worse. Kansas was . . .

Bloody Kansas.

Riding with Quantrill and Anderson was murder and robbing and rape and torture. . . .

After drinking dinner, the patrol moves out, twenty men in all. Captain John Slocum has been ordered,

*by Quantrill himself, to kill a Yankee landowner.
The house must be burned ... anything not burned
can be taken by the men ... the women are to be
used before they are killed, if possible. The men
always insisted on that.*

*At first, the pounding hooves drive out all
thought, and that's good. But later, closer to the
farm where Charles and Jack McCarthy blithely
rest this night, the patrol slows and begins to move
carefully, silently. Then it's possible for a man to
think and reflect on what it is he's about to do.
Captain Slocum knows that the McCarthys are
wealthy Yankees; he knows that they are tough and
hard, but have a reputation for dealing fair with
their workers and in their business with others. It
doesn't matter. A Confederate planter had been
burned out the week before ... the pickings have
been lean and the men are restless and the Mc-
Carthys are Yankees. They're nothing but farmers,
not soldiers. Slocum knows they will be cut down,
and he is the one who will do it.*

*Just before dawn, Slocum and his riders come
up to the farm and the outbuildings of the McCarthy family. It is dark and quiet—even the birds are
silent yet. The raiders halt at the edge of the woods
just before the land cleared by the hard work and
the strong hands of these simple enemies.*

*Slocum looks around at the hard, excited faces
of his men. His sharp green eyes know them for
the terrors that they are; there's not a decent man
among them ... except, perhaps, for himself.
Lately, he has begun to wonder very seriously
about himself. The men sport every combination*

and variety of garment possible. All, including Slo-cum, are filthy. But every pistol and rifle and knife is clean. They sit, waiting, waiting for Slocum's command. What would happen, Slocum wonders for a brief fleeting moment, if I ordered them to turn around and return to camp? What would hap-pen? Slocum knows he is too much of a coward to do that; he has no power to stop this. If he doesn't go along, he will be swept away, he knows.

This captain—all regret and misgiving locked away, ready to be brought out and examined years later—raises his arm and lets it fall. Before the arm falls, nineteen men, screaming lustily, ride pell-mell toward the house and barn and sleeping peo-ple. Slocum can only follow wearily.

Charles McCarthy, roused from sleepily milking a cow, runs out of the barn, and is shot through the head—his shotgun left leaning against the wall. The first two raiders into the house are shot by his brother, Jack, who is standing fearlessly in his nightclothes on the rather elaborate curving stair-way that is the symbol of his family's pride and success. One of the men he's shot, a Missourian distantly related to the James brothers, is killed outright; the other is so badly wounded, Slocum must put him out of his misery later in the morning. Shots ring out from the second floor, finding targets in the milling crowd below—Slocum's horse is one of the victims. Despite this brave beginning, how-ever, the guerrillas quickly kill Jack McCarthy— he's cut down by the third man into the house. Slocum watches the body, riddled with bullets, roll down the stairs leaving a trail of blood on each

*step. With a whoop, the rest of the men run into
the house and begin fanning out, looking for loot,
running up the stairs, breaking and destroying anything they won't be able to carry away with them.
Those who move up onto the second floor are
wary—there is a rifleman somewhere on this floor.
And where are the women? Both McCarthy brothers have wives; one of them is reputed to be fair
to look on.*

*Two hired hands, mistakenly believing that they
could remain uninvolved, stupidly hoping that
they could walk away, surrender, and are quickly
hanged. Their bodies are set afire by torches, and
the sweet, greasy smoke of burning flesh is blown
into Slocum's face.*

*In his mind's merciless eye, Slocum sees himself
watching a short distance from the house, envel-
oped by the smell of his innocent victims—like one
of those Old Testament sacrifices, Slocum thinks
suddenly.*

*The wife of one of the Yankee brothers—Slocum
never did find out which one—has been the rifleman at the second-floor window. The other wife has
the good fortune to be away. Perhaps the fact that
the woman there has killed one horse and wounded
three men accounts for how badly she will be
treated by Slocum's men. Wounded in the face by
gunfire from below, she is quickly disarmed by the
four ruffians who'd run up to the second floor. John
can hear her screams of outrage and pain as she
is raped by the men he has brought here to her.
Raucous laughter and shouts are everywhere
about. Breaking glass and crashes fill the dawn.*

*The burning bodies of the two hired men are jerk-
ing in great arching spasms—apparently the
nooses hadn't been tied properly—almost, it seems,
in time to poor Mrs. McCarthy's screams and cries.*

*"Captain, there's no one else around. Want us
to start to burn the house when the men upstairs
are done? Captain? Captain?"*

*Standing aside and apart from all this, but still
connected to everything that is happening, Slocum
cannot answer. He can only watch. He is unable
to stop anything or to help anyone, including himself.*

*Sometime later that year, he will not be able to
stand aside in silence; Quantrill himself will put a
bullet into his body, leaving him for dead.*

Bloody Kansas.

Slocum looked around. Dawn had broken. He was
damned tired of thinking and damned sick of going
around and around in his head, unable to let go of
his remorse. He hated thinking about the war, and
he'd just wasted a whole night chewing through it
again. He began to fear that he was unable to move
on, that he was unwilling, somehow, to change.

With a string of curses, he broke the meager
camp he'd made and set out again, deeper into the
mountains.

As the day began, John found his mood once more
start to lighten. If only he could keep it going and
not slide back. He kept telling himself that he was
tough, that he'd always been able to survive by

adapting to any hard situation, to any circumstance; he'd always been able to overcome any obstacle or ride around it. As he rode on that morning, oblivious again to the surrounding world, Slocum kept telling himself that he could turn things around, that he could once more walk with his head held high. He wanted so much to be confident again. He hated the way he'd been living his life these past few weeks. He realized that he might have been hating his life for years without knowing it, and that he might have to make some big changes. Lately, his spirits had been so low that he couldn't think straight.

Hell. I've hardly been able to think at all.

Slocum wanted to believe that it was just a matter of time before he sorted everything out. He decided that he wanted to make it sooner rather than later, and that it was time that he stopped moaning and whining. It was time to think straight about the business.

As soon as he reached that decision, Slocum felt less worried, less fearful, and began, as a first step, to scout the country he was riding through. He had to find a good camping spot. He made a second decision—he was going to have to regain his old instincts; if he didn't, his bones would be bleaching under the sun in no time.

Early in life, Slocum had learned to be an excellent woodsman and tracker. Throughout his life he'd improved on those skills until his senses had been joined by a sixth sense. He concentrated those senses and skills now, feeling a rush of the old joy in being alive in a place where that in itself was something of an accomplishment. He spent the rest of the morning and the early part of the afternoon looking for the place where he would rest, hunt, and figure everything out. He was looking for a good campsite—a safe place where he was unlikely to be bothered by other humans. He was looking for a place that looked right, that *felt* right. A place where he could have some peace and quiet.

He hadn't found it by late afternoon. The general area was right: high mountains covered with aspen and plenty of game—though he hadn't been cutting much sign lately; that was funny. He just hadn't found the place where he wanted to stop yet. Slocum was getting impatient; he wanted to get on with it. *Well, if I don't find it today, I'll find it tomorrow.*

Slocum was restless, anxious. He felt as if he was waiting for something, on the verge of something. It was going to happen any minute. Something's coming, John realized with surprise. He knew it. And it felt good. It would feel even better once it actually happened. Then he would be doing something instead of waiting, instead of wandering lost and confused. He understood why he had been so restless now. *Something's coming.*

He rode on. He realized that it had gotten very silent, that it had been silent for some time. *Quiet. No birds. No wind.* Everything seemed so still. Up a rock-strewn slope covered with trees . . . a curve to the right, and he saw the cabin off in the distance. The trees thinned out some between himself and the cabin; the ground was covered with white flowers, like a carpet.

There's no trail, no tracks, no human sign at all. Strange. Haven't seen any animal tracks either, none.

He stopped his horse, a little disappointed; he really didn't want to deal with anyone right now. Slocum considered going around the cabin, bypassing it completely. *Sun's getting low.*

An owl hooted and his horse seemed nervous, shifting and snorting. Slocum quieted him and abruptly decided to take a closer look. The owl hooted again.

As he approached slowly, cautiously, Slocum surveyed the area. *It's a good spot.* The slope was covered with trees—but not enough to afford much cover. *They must have seen me by now.* There was a huge outcropping just behind the cabin, so there was really only one way to approach. John saw a small waterfall in the rocks, there was water too.

Turning around quickly, he saw the ground falling away, the lower slopes of the mountain thick with trees in the fading light. It was a beautiful place. The light was still good up this high. He could see other mountain ranges in the distance, and rivers, and valleys. Cloud formations lumbered across the sky. Slocum remembered his favorite childhood game—he and his brother would try to make out shapes in the clouds. Looks like a wagon train over there, he thought. And that one looks to be a man with a long rifle, and those are two people at his feet. He shook his head; he was letting his imagination run away with him. The owl hooted and was joined by another. His horse pranced sideways and tried to turn, but John quickly got him straightened out. He could feel the great flank muscles shivering between his legs. *That damned bird's beginning to get on my nerves too.* He looked around sharply, searching the trees, but couldn't locate anything. *Now, that's funny. An owl—in the daytime? Never heard a' no owl hooting in the daytime.*

The cabin up ahead waited. Slocum urged his horse forward and off to the side. Coming up on the structure obliquely, he saw that the whole back portion was collapsed; the place had to be deserted. From the front, at that distance, it had seemed whole. Slocum had *felt* that it was occupied.

The wind started to pick up as he moved closer and closer. Blowing leaves and flowers and undergrowth crackled under his horse's hooves. Unable to make a complete circuit because of the rock just up against the back of the tumbled-down structure, Slocum rode his agitated animal around as much as he could. Surveying the cabin from a distance of ten feet, he could see that it had been gutted by fire.

Must have started in the back—front wall's pretty much intact.

It looked to have been a sturdy structure, and Slocum wondered about the man who'd built it. He seemed to have been a clever and practical man. He'd chosen an easily defended site, with ready water and a spectacular view; the house was well built and showed off the man's skill. Slocum looked it over with admiration—he was so envious of a man who could manage his life like Gerry the bartender, and of this man, who could build something strong. Slocum estimated that the fire had destroyed the house about one year before, maybe more.

Dismounting and tying his horse to a tree with tight knots, Slocum made a closer examination. The rising wind whipped leaves and debris against his legs, and long, thin white flowers rubbed his ankles. He had to hold his hat with one hand as he walked up to the cabin. He looked inside and decided that he could pitch a lean-to against the remaining wall, keep out the wind. *Looks to be cold tonight.* He started in clearing space, and was so intent that he paid little attention to the owl's hoots.

Having just gotten a good fire going, Slocum suddenly felt like he was being watched. He could feel eyes, almost like a hand gently caressing his back. He straightened. Slowly he turned and moved casually away from the fire, green eyes boring into the gathering darkness around him. All about were little sounds, the ticking noises of things being borne by the wind, and the sound of water dripping in the little fall.

Or it could be someone sneaking around.

Slocum was intently staring, to locate whoever it was who'd snuck up on him. His horse was stamping and blowing, and three owls seemed to be calling back and forth just off to his right.

Goddamn. A man can't hear anything with all this racket.

Pulling out his pistol and calmly thumbing back the hammer, Slocum cautiously moved toward the owls. The darkness was finally moving up and around the cabin like a mist, making it difficult to make out shapes even a few feet away. Everything seemed threatening. John slowly swung his gaze all about, positive there was someone near. There always seemed to be *something* just outside his vision, or just at the edge of his hearing.

For more than an hour, he prowled slowly, often stopping suddenly, holding still for minutes on end, trying to listen through the wind and the noises of the wind. His nerves were stretched tight by the waiting. Searching through the darkness, probing with all his senses, he would wheel quickly, hoping to catch the lurking presence. Slocum felt alive to the tips of his fingers and toes.

Finally, he gave up, still feeling like there was something or someone around him somewhere. He squatted before the fire, took out the makin's, and began rolling a cigarette, still a little nervous, though he didn't spill a shred of the tobacco. Pretty good trick, he thought, in this wind.

He continued to feel that gentle touch on his back, but dragging deeply on the thin smoke, he resolved that he wasn't going to go spooking himself or running off in a panic. *If there is someone around, he's got to be pretty damned good. And if he's that damned good, he'd have my damned scalp by now. Best to wait this out and see what happens.*

John stayed hunched by the fire, finished the first cigarette, then rolled and smoked two more. When he heard the owl, he stood again, drew his revolver again, and moved back into the darkness. Quickly moving out of the flickering circle of firelight, he roamed through the woods, gingerly placing each step, keeping low, trying desperately to probe the darkness. He used every trick, every device he'd learned in a lifetime on the frontier to flush the intruder. He spent another hour like this, again in vain. There *couldn't* be anyone else around, yet all his instincts told him there was.

He dropped his pistol back into its holster, and walked noisily back to the shelter and warmth of his camp. "You all can come out whenever you want to. I'm gonna try and get me some sleep."

This was ridiculous, he thought, as he rolled a thin little smoke. It was too late to move his camp—besides, he was scaring himself; how could anyone be hiding out there? *I'll move at first light— if I still have my hair.*

John settled down to rest, knowing that he'd never be able to sleep, confident that his visitor would show himself sooner or later.

I'll wait up, even if it takes all damned night.

He was asleep in a few moments.

In his dream he dreamt he was someone else. . . .

7

His hands were on his wife's breasts. He felt her body sway in the grass beneath him as he gently squeezed the small, firm mounds. The two lovers lay behind the newly built cabin, a few feet from a pool of clear water. Her open mouth slid across his neck and cheeks and ears in slow circular patterns. For a little while, his heart and mind were completely at peace. He could hear every drip of the perfectly timed waterfall, each blade of grass touching his body, every single inch of his flesh against her and in her. He felt calm and strong, and full of love.

I'm Rick White.

His hands moved up into her waist-length black hair, guiding her head from one place to another, then down her sides and flanks to cup the wonderful little cheeks of her ass, guiding her hips to move in time with his own. He continued to slide in and out of her in long, slow strokes while her hands moved over his back and down along his buttocks, and caressed the tops of his thighs.

She kept whispering, "Rick, Rick, Rick . . ." over and over, until the sound of his name couldn't be separated from the water and the birds and the sighing of the warm breeze.

In the crazy way that dreams make perfect sense, Slocum had the feeling that he was looking out through another person's eyes, that his hands and body belonged to someone else . . . that he was living another life but he was still himself. The other life he was living was Rick White's. In the crazy assurance of this dream, John Slocum knew that he was living Rick White's life through Rick. It was so real, it wasn't like a dream at all.

Rick could feel White's body; it was tall (taller than Slocum's six feet one inch); it was a thin, wiry frame, but tight with muscle. He was covered with scars and he remembered every fight, every accident, every blow and cut; it was his pride that every wound he'd received in a fight was on the front of his body . . . just like Alexander the Great, Rick liked to say. And Slocum knew somehow that in his childhood (Rick's childhood) he had been taught the classics—that he'd enjoyed Xenophon and Plutarch, Caesar and Herodotus.

Slocum had a quick flash of a young boy sitting on the stairs of a rich home, sun streaming through stained-glass windows, reading and daydreaming. It was all so long ago—in another life. Everyone he knew called him "White," except for Rose, his wife. She called him "Rick." He thought of himself as Rick—that was what his parents had called their pride and joy, their only surviving child. They had loved him and cared for him and encouraged him. Before they died they had given him the great gift of self-confidence. It was a gift Slocum could appreciate and envy. It was a gift that he too had been given by his own parents . . . but he had mislaid it somewhere along the way.

Rose's hands clutching his long blond (almost white) hair brought him out of these thoughts to more physical and immediate concerns. Her wetness and trembling pulled him back into the overwhelming sensations of lovemaking.

He was so hard he thought he would burst. When Rose brought her legs tight up around his waist, pushing him deeper into her body, he shouted and came in several long, emptying bursts.

Resting his weight on both elbows and forearms so as not to crush her, Rick brought his mouth onto hers, sucking at her tongue noisily, grinding his hips gently, moving quietly in her.

Sometime later, the both of them, spent, but somehow exhilarated, separated their wet bodies. They lay on their backs in the cool grass, looking up at the billowed clouds in an impossibly blue sky. For a long time, they tried to see shapes in the clouds, laughing when they couldn't agree on what each thought they saw.

Through Rick's sharp, gray eyes, Slocum studied Rose. She was dark-skinned and small-boned—tiny almost—with powerful little hands and tiny doll's feet. Rick could cover her small, hard breasts completely with a cupped hand. Her hips were full— when he was in her, Rick said, it was like rocking in a cradle. Though only her legs were muscular, she was physically strong and capable of great endurance. When they had moved up onto the mountain, Rick remembered, Rose had helped him build the cabin—he had been surprised at the weight she could lift and carry, at how she could work all day without tiring.

Studying her features, Slocum decided—though Rick would have disagreed—that she wasn't what you would call pretty; her face was too wide, her cheekbones too prominent, her broken nose too large. It was the eyes, those almond-shaped, black eyes, sparkling with intelligence and vivacity, that made her beautiful. It was the graceful way she walked and stood and carried herself that made her wonderful to watch. And that hair. Black, thick, shining—it cascaded down her back. She took great pains with the care of it; it was her pride. When they made love, Rick knew she would want him to thrust his hands into the mass of it, playing with strands and stroking it as if her hair were warm flesh.

Rick loved the woman. She accepted him and loved him as well. The person he was when he was with her made him happy to be alive. She'd adapted to their new mountain home easily; initially, Rick had worried that his Cheyenne wife would miss the plains, but she'd said that even though she loved the flat ground because it was her childhood home, she would love the mountains because they were her adult home and the home she would make with Rick. Besides, like Rick, Rose loved solitude, and the mountains seemed to draw those who needed to live apart, those who were tough and strong-willed. Rose was certainly tough— back when he'd done some scouting for the U.S. Cavalry, Rick had seen her dissuade more than a few randy soldiers who'd made the mistake of thinking that this quiet woman was an easily plucked little fruit. She was surprisingly adept at wielding and throwing the wicked little knife she always carried. And strong-willed ... well, like Rick, once she made up her mind she was almost impossible to move; she was clever enough to figure out just about anything too.

Slocum wished he'd found a woman as capable as Rose, one so adept at bringing out the best in her mate ... things might have been different for him. The very hope of finding one was reason enough to live, he thought with some gratitude.

Rick got to his feet, threw his head back, and stretched until he heard muscle and tendon pop and crack. Reaching down, he said, "C'mon, let's walk a bit."

Taking his hand, Rose got up. "Yes. On our land."

They walked off, leaving their clothes and weapons behind.

There were birds everywhere: on the rocks, in the trees, hopping on the ground. Though their calls, songs, and chattering seemed chaotic at first, it made a sort of background music for Rick and Rose's walk. There were plenty of animals too. In full view, seemingly unafraid—squirrels, deer, even bear—all manner of beast seemed drawn to the woods around the new cabin.

The man and woman walked, hand in hand, through this abundance, talking of the future they would build. The soft flesh of the earth, leaves, pine needles, dirt and stone, was beneath their feet, and a warm breeze blew steadily.

"Let's have a lot of kids."

Rose smiled. "Many. A strong son first."

Around them the sun shone through the trees. They walked slowly, watching the animals and birds, talking about their ways and antics. They stood a long time at a spot where they could look out over the tops of the trees to mountains standing tall in the distance. The air was so clear, Rick knew he would just have to reach out his hand to touch them.

"I want to spend the rest of my life here," Rose said, squeezing her husband's hand in hers. "This will be a good place for our children, and for their children."

Above, a hawk swooped and dived, and a brief squeal rang through the forest. The birds and animals, silenced for just a second, resumed their noise.

"They won't have to worry about being crowded, like them out there." Rick motioned off into the distance with his head. "Here they'll be able to breathe their own air."

He wanted nothing more than to be left alone with the family and life he would build here—like the cabin he'd built further up the mountain. He wanted nothing more than the chance to build a life with the woman at his side.

Watching her, he wondered, as always, what

there was in him that made her love him so. She was so graceful and he was so clumsy. She was beautiful; he was ugly next to her grace and beauty.

They did this often, in between chores. After making love by the pool, they'd walk through the woods, watching the animals and the birds, noting the subtle changes in the land they called their own. Usually Rick carried a rifle with him and Rose wore a belt with her sheathed knife—even if they left their clothes behind. But they had become so comfortable, they felt so safe in their paradise, that they sometimes forgot. It was so beautiful, and their hands and bodies and minds were so calmed by their loving, that Slocum, from his vantage point, could see their guard had relaxed just a little bit. Though he slept, he worried about Rick.

Their paradise was surrounded by a dangerous world.

Rick and Rose walked back through the trees, listening to the wind rustling the leaves. Walking around their one-room cabin, they decided to look at it from all angles. They discussed where to put an addition for the children they knew would come, planning for the years they would spend together.

Rick had built well; their house was solid. Long, sturdy logs were pegged together (he'd searched the forest for just the right wood, picking only the best and most durable materials), with stone and mud stuffed into the chinks and smoothed out while still drying. The inside walls would be draped, come winter, with furs. The front door was attached by metal hinges, and Rick had even built a stone fireplace and chimney.

There's magic in his hands, Rose thought with a smile.

The floor was hardpacked earth and Rose had arranged all their tools, coats, weapons, and utensils neatly on pegs driven into the walls. Their clothes and food were kept in wooden chests and colorfully decorated leather parfleches.

Rick had not neglected defense when he built his home. There were several covered slits on the wall that could open to allow a line of fire on attackers. The door was sturdy and could withstand many heavy blows, and the windows could be closed off with thick wooden shutters secured by heavy bars. Rick had even constructed a cunning little trapdoor at the rear of the structure—a sally port that could be used to surprise attackers, or could be used for a quiet escape.

Looking around, Rick was satisfied with what he had done; his home would last. Soon, he knew, they would need more room. Maybe he'd add a sleeping loft looking down on the main room, as well as an extension . . . if the extension were placed on the opposite side of the house, and he could get the loft high enough, its window could be used to fire down on attackers. He began to think about where the loft could be raised, using his imagination to visualize what it would look like. He began to calculate how much work would be needed to open up and raise the roof, how much lumber would have to be cut, how the lumber would have to be dressed. He knew it would take a good deal of time, but the pleasure it would bring to him and the woman would be well worth it.

Rick enjoyed this kind of figuring; it seemed his brain worked at a greater speed when he approached a problem logically. It gave him great pleasure to be able to break a job down into pieces and arrange the pieces into separate smaller jobs.

Slocum, sleeping, was awed by the ideas and calculations that flew through Rick's mind. Ideas appeared, coalesced, and became workable plans in a blink.

Slocum had once been able to act like that— when he'd apprehended danger, he'd act without thinking. When you're really good at something, like fighting, bulding, or music, your mind seems to be able to skip steps.

I can't do that anymore. Slocum feared, in his dreaming, that all the instinct, skill, and tricks that had so often saved his life and delivered him from so many tight spots were gone forever. With his sleeping eye, he saw his diminished self trying to survive; with his sleeping heart, he mourned his lost youth and fading skills. He prayed like he'd never prayed before that he'd be able to get some of those skills back. Just for a moment, he wondered what the price for regaining those skills would be.

Though Rick was deep in thought, seeing only the steps needed to add a loft and another room, Slocum watched Rose. The look in her face spoke of love and admiration. She knew what her husband was thinking, what he was working at, and she loved him for it.

Slocum could see that. In the dream, Slocum's vision was clear. The way she was looking at Rick made John wish he were in love again, made him want to be loved. Slocum, drinking in these two lives, wanted, more than anything he'd ever wanted before, to have the weight lifted from his heart.

Indians would have told him that his life, his spirit journey, had been blocked, and only the most dire consequences would result. John realized the truth of that—he could see how he'd suffered since Cahill was killed . . . since he'd killed Cahill.

No. It was before that even. Before that, he'd been directionless—God only knows how long— and he'd been dreading every day. He'd told himself that he was tired, that he was worn out, that he needed a rest . . . but it was more than that. Slocum needed a direction; he needed to find a way to regain all the good that had been drained out of him by trying to survive in a hard world.

Once again, he marveled at the clarity of his thinking—for months he'd been feeling sorry for himself, trying to figure out what was wrong. Now, in one night's dreaming, he'd seemed to figure out more than he'd been able to do—even with Gerry helping him—since this all began.

This was a damn strange dream. He hoped he remembered it in the morning.

When you thought about it, life was pretty damn strange.

Rick stood a long time looking at the house he'd built so recently. Life was pretty damn strange— already he was looking to change it.

Rose squeezed his hand. "Come. Let's finish our chores."

He nodded and let her lead him into the cabin.

For weeks afterward, Rick White sat and looked at his house: occasionally he'd turn and look into the woods. It got so he wasn't good for chores. He'd just sit and think.

Rose knew what he was doing—he was sitting and figuring exactly what needed to be done to enlarge the cabin. He was figuring which trees to cut and where they'd be used, and how to dress them. She knew what was going on in that head. She saw him calculating each step of the process in detail. He didn't discuss any of this with her yet, but she knew.

When he was done, when he had every last step firm in his mind, he'd sit her down and explain the whole thing at length, step by step. As soon as he made her see it like he did, the work would begin. It usually went exactly the way he'd explained it.

When he was deep in thought, while he was puzzling the thing out, she wouldn't disturb him for anything—not even to tell him her news. She was sure now. She did all the chores that he neglected— even though some of it was heavy work. She never complained. She could do anything a man could do.

And one thing more.

Just as she knew he would, Rick came to her with his detailed plans. She sat and only half-listened as he explained what he would do and how long each step would take. Finally, as he was nearing what she hoped would be the end, she could contain herself no longer.

"Rick. I'm going to have a baby."

Rick continued talking and explaining for a few seconds, then stopped in mid-sentence. He looked at her seriously for a few short heartbeats. He looked around at their mountain, at their home, smelling of rock and fir and flower. Hands on hips, he began to laugh, realizing with great joy what a rich and happy man he was.

"A baby," he said. Holding his arms out to Rose, he hugged her, then started to waltz her around the cabin, knocking over anything that got in their lurching path. Both of them were laughing now. Both of them, looking onto each other's eyes, knew that they were happier than they'd ever been. Each knew that this—their life together—was what they'd been born for.

Slocum, sleeping, watching, unable to blink or look away, felt that happiness. He liked Rick and Rose White, these creatures of his reverie. He knew they couldn't be real—he knew that even while he observed them so intimately. But John Slocum felt they were alive, and he admired these two; he admired their courage and independence. He was glad they had each other's love; their faith in the dreams they dreamed made him happy. More than that, their dreams gave him hope. Slocum had been stuck in an evil past for so long that he was slowly but surely killing himself. When he'd realized what he was doing he'd forgotten how to stop—he'd forgotten that he *could* stop. All he was seeing were his mistakes and failures—it was poisoning him.

Looking at the world through the fresh eyes of Rick White showed Slocum just how much he was missing—and how much he was crippling himself.

If I keep this up, I'll kill myself before anyone else gets the chance.

There was another part of John Slocum that hated Rick and Rose White, however. That part of him was furious and resentful that they walked together while he walked alone and lonely; that part of John Slocum was jealous because they'd found what eluded him, because they'd found what he wasn't good enough to ever have.

It was an eerie feeling—loving and hating the same person.

Suddenly, he knew that he could survive—and prosper even—if he let his anger and impatience command him. He could defeat his whining ways and his helplessness through fury. He would become like a mad dog . . . but he wouldn't be a victim anymore—he would make others become the victims. It was tempting—he had so much resentment and fear . . . it would be easy . . . and didn't he already have a head start? He often found himself on the verge of that kind of madness as it was. It would be a sure way to regain his power.

There was another way, his conscience, which never slept, told him; it was harder, it would take longer . . . he could use his head, he could follow what he believed was the right path. His conscience told him that it wasn't what you got out of life, but how you went about getting it, and how you waited for it. It was all in the waiting.

Slocum's sleeping body tossed and turned in the

ruins of the cabin as he went over all this. Embers hissed and glowed and died, and were blown back into life by the relentless wind. His unconscious whispers were echoed by the cries of three owls perched on the walls and burnt rafters. The dark forest surrounding Slocum teemed with life; Slocum's small voice was joined by the wind rising and the sounds of predators and their victims.

While John moved, increasingly restless, in sleep, his inner dreaming eye closed for a moment. He came close to moving back into the real world. But it was as if the forest around the tumbledown cabin sensed that he was suspended between the two worlds, and held its breath. The owls fell silent. Even the wind died for a few moments. No animals hunted, and none died . . . for a few short minutes all was still. Nothing stirred.

Slocum slowly fell back into a deep slumber.

His inner eye opened, his inner ears heard again . . . and he continued to dream. He dreamed he was Rick White. . . .

It must have been a month later. No one but Slocum saw, but Rose White was pregnant. No one but Rick and Slocum would have noticed; she was carrying small and her stomach barely bulged. But Rick knew, and when they made love by the pool, he was very gentle now. He would run his hands slowly over her belly, and down between her legs, caressing her inner thighs before moving his finger into her in slow stages. When he entered her and his shaft moved in and out of her body, he no longer thrust; he moved carefully, slowly.

Though he understood that it was too early, he felt he could touch his unborn child while loving his wife.

When, openmouthed, he kissed her long and slow, he felt he was breathing life into the waiting child—the child who could grow up to be as strong and independent as his mother and father. Though the two never spoke of it, Rose sensed her husband's feelings—she grasped his shoulders and seemed to try to pull him ever deeper into her, to pull his strength into the child, wanting the baby to accept the gift of his strength—strength she knew the child would need in a hard world.

When they were done, resting by the pool of clean, clear water, Rose said, "I have never been happier."

"Me neither." Rick moved to stand, but she put out a hand to stop him. "I want you to know how happy you have made me."

Jesus Lord, Slocum thought. He could feel their joy.

"You've made me as happy," Rick replied. "And it's going to get better when them pretty little babies start comin' and I can run some horses over in the mountain pasture—"

Her hand stopped him again. "Even if the worst happened, *we* would still be."

"What are you talkin' about? What do you think is going to happen?" He looked at her seriously. "Did you have one of them spirit dreams again?"

"No, husband. I have not had a spirit dream. I dream only of your hands, and our child." She placed outspread fingers over her lower stomach, and smiled. "I just mean to say that our loving would make us happy even if the world went against us."

Rick put his hands over hers and frowned. "Well, yeah. But don't be talking about bad things happening, or some of them spirits might be listening."

They looked at each other a long while. Rick wondered what was going on in her head. It could be anything, he knew. She was different, she wasn't like anyone he'd ever imagined . . . she wasn't like anyone who'd ever been. When he'd first met her, he'd taken her silence for surliness, for anger. He'd learned that her silence came from the intense way she observed the world and everything that went on around her, from the deep way she considered everything. Her silence came from the long years of wandering alone. She barely spoke of those years, or her childhood, or of the Cheyenne she came from—even to Rick. Her husband wasn't the kind to try and pry it out of her. After he came to know and love her, the past didn't matter so much—only the present and the future were important.

Only the present and the future . . . John Slocum, trapped in his dream of another man's life, heard that thought and it rang like a dinner bell.

Rick was a little uneasy. Like him, Rose had highly developed senses of smell and hearing. She also had an additional sense of knowing when danger was near, or of being able to act an instant before danger surprised her. Rick recognized that—many people on the frontier had this extra sense . . . the ones that survived, at least. But Rose had one more ability that gave Rick pause. Sometimes, Rose could tell what was going to happen in the future. He'd seen a few that could do that—mostly Indians. Usually it came to her in a dream—she'd say then that she'd had a spirit dream. Sometimes, she'd look up and tell him what was going to happen—and it would happen. It might be a day later, or three days, or a year, but it *would* happen just like she said. Like all such medicine, you never knew *when* she would be able to use it; it just came on its own.

Once, just after they'd met and begun living together, just after he'd quit scouting for the cavalry, a group of settlers in a five-wagon party wanted to hire Rick to lead them through the mountains— wanted to pay more than the going rate too. They were led by a stringy old bird—from New England somewhere, judging from his sparse talk—named Hezekiah. The old man just walked up to Rick, without a howdy-do, and said, "Heard you're the only reliable scout around. You'll do." They dickered on the price awhile, but Rick *was* the only reliable scout around at the time, and Hezekiah didn't want to wait.

Rick figured to be well paid for a few days of easy riding. But Rose walked up behind him, looked deep into his eyes, and said, "My man will not be able to work for you."

Both men looked at her in surprise.

"Who in damnation is she?" Hezekiah demanded.

"My, uh, wife," White answered.

"You always let your woman do your talkin' for ye?"

Rose wouldn't look at Hezekiah. Rick felt her hand trembling on his arm. He looked at her, then at the old man. "I won't be able to go," Rick finally said.

Hezekiah spat. "Let a woman tell you what to do . . . maybe you ain't the man for us after all." He walked away, muttering.

Rick turned to Rose, frowning. She was watching Hezekiah's retreating back. She said, "That man would have sunk his ax in your head."

Rick didn't say anything.

About a week later, one of the wagons in the New England party returned. One wagon and six people were all that were left. Hezekiah Bennington had gotten up one morning before dawn and decided to take his party to heaven . . . he'd used an ax. The first person he'd killed was the scout who'd hired on in Rick's place.

Rick never questioned her medicine after that. He decided it was best to be cautious. He was cautious now.

Naked, the two lovers walked back to their cabin. The somber mood seemed to have fled—Rick thought about building the new additions. He was looking forward to the hard physical work, but most of all, he was anticipating hearing his first-born's joyful cries. Rose thought of being able to hold her child and her husband in her arms at the same time.

It was a bright, clear afternoon, warm. It was a

day full of the sights and sounds and smells of the mountain and the forest. Rick and Rose White would never be happier.

A little while later, after dressing, Rick was chopping wood. Suddenly he stopped in mid-stroke. Senses long sharpened by life on the prairie and in the mountains told him that something was different . . . not right. He didn't hear anything, or see anything, or smell anything—but there was . . . *something*.

"Rose," he called softly. She appeared immediately, holding one of their rifles, just inside the doorway into the cabin.

"Rick?"

Hefting the ax, he said, "Throw me the rifle. Get another for yourself."

Without a word, she disappeared into the dim interior. A moment later, he heard her voice. "Catch."

Still looking around and sniffing the air, Rick caught the rifle in one hand. In another smooth motion, he dropped the ax and loped into the woods. "Keep an eye out. Listen for me." He was gone in an eyeblink.

As soon as he was swallowed by the trees, she came out of the cabin and crouched behind the woodpile. Her head went up and she too sniffed and watched and listened. She could detect nothing, but now, she also felt that something was not quite right around her.

The wind sighed—that was as it should be. She could hear birds—a dozen or more behind the cabin, a crow in the trees to her left—no danger there. Rose's senses moved out around her . . . a small four-footed animal in the brush up ahead of her—that didn't account for her unease. Horses in the corral . . . Everything she saw around her— brush trees, house, woodpile, shadows—was normal. She saw no one.

She used the old trick of not looking at anything in particular. She let her eyes see everything, let her ears hear everything; she let herself go, trying to feel everything around her. If something didn't belong, she'd realize it.

Rick had disappeared completely—not a sign of him.

Rose waited a long time. She changed her position often, and never stopped concentrating her senses. She could detect nothing. Her secret sense had also stopped warning her. Though it never paid to ignore her inner warnings, they *were* sometimes false alarms.

About twenty feet away, Rick stepped out from behind a tree and walked over to her casually. His wariness was gone. He shrugged. "Couldn't find no sign. Sorry I got you all worked up."

"It's better you get me worked up for no reason, than not get me worked up when there is a reason."

Rick smiled. "Reckon so."

That evening, an old friend came to visit.

Just before nightfall, when they were about to have their evening meal, Rick and Rose looked up at the same time. A few minutes later, a horse could be heard moving up the path toward them. Both had loaded rifles close to hand, though they realized that whoever was coming was taking pains to be heard.

Slocum, who shared the survival senses of his dream partners, was alarmed.

A horse and rider came into view. The Whites stood quickly, as soon as they recognized their visitor.

Slocum, through Rick's eyes, saw a huge horse, seemingly a draught horse, carrying an older man. It became evident that the man was huge. Slocum judged him to be in his fifties—maybe late forties; it was hard to tell since he was hidden by grime and worn clothes. His hair was completely gray, hanging in greasy, tangled strands down past his shoulders; his beard was as long, and as gray and dirty. The man rode up and dismounted without saying a word, though he smiled slightly.

Slocum, through Rick, saw a man about seven inches over six feet. Filthy, stained buckskins covered the long body, and seemed several sizes too small. Slocum wondered when they'd last been cleaned . . . *probably when they were last taken off him—which appears to be never.* The man's hard, bunchy muscles and slim body were clearly outlined.

Rick and Rose knew the man, and knew him well; and John Slocum was introduced to Hal Tudor. Tudor was a man no one was likely to forget.

Rick had scouted with him when he rode for the cavalry, and knew—from personal experience— that he was tough and vicious. On more than one occasion, Rick had seen him proudly display the scalps he'd taken—there were over forty of them.

Tudor could tell you when and how he'd come by each and every one. The Whites knew he was clever, quick, and deadly, incredibly strong and incredibly lucky at everything except gambling.

Tudor smiled at his hosts.

Whew! Not what you'd call good-looking, thought Slocum wryly.

Nearly all the man's teeth were missing, and those that remained were pointed and stained. His nose was mashed flat, and when he put up a hand in greeting, Slocum realized that his hands were like huge paws—big even for a man of that size— covered with hard layers of callus. The nails were long—*Good Lord, could they be sharpened?*—and were caked under with dirt.

Tudor's giant, bare feet completed the bizarre picture. Filthy, like the rest of him, they clutched the earth. Like a vulture's talons, the skin was cracked and grayish. Rick had seen Tudor cover his feet only during the worst winters. Usually, they were kept bare even in the cold and ice.

Slocum was well traveled and had seen much, but he'd never seen anyone like Hal Tudor . . . he was glad it was a dream. *Good thing I didn't meet up with this hombre when I was drinking—even Gerry would have a tough time with the likes of him.*

The Whites, already somewhat on edge from their experience earlier in the afternoon, were none too happy to play the host to Hal Tudor. Though Rick had scouted with him for a few years, he'd never trusted him . . . especially around Rose, or around a deck of cards. Fact was, the last time

they'd seen each other—about seven months before—Rick had won a good deal of money from
Tudor. The grizzled old man had looked murder
while Rick had swept the coins into a pouch. Rick
had had a mind to check his backtrail for a while
after that.

Rose knew that Tudor's eyes had always followed her wherever she went—they still did,
though he tried to hide it. He always seemed to
prefer the camp followers and prostitutes that went
everywhere soldiers went . . . but Rose knew he
fancied her. She had expected him to make his in-
tentions known, and she knew he would be one of
those that did not like being refused—she had sunk
her teeth and her knife into more than one of that
kind; she'd even shot one. This Tudor would be
very difficult, very dangerous. When Rick had
come into her life there wasn't room for anyone
else, and Tudor had seemed to look elsewhere.

No one had thought about how much anger and
resentment he carried in his heart.

And there he was now, with his big, dirty hand
up in greeting. Standing at their doorstep.

No, the Whites were none too overjoyed to see
him. No, they didn't trust him.

Both realized, without having to say it out loud,
that their experience in the afternoon was a warning
about Tudor's coming—perhaps he'd even spied
on them before approaching openly. But neither
Rick nor Rose would turn away a guest if they
could help it. Besides, like all loving couples, they
were proud of the life they'd built together and
wanted to show off. Unless Tudor threatened them,

he would be welcome—even though their instincts warned them.

Neither Rick nor Rose would rest easily, however, while Hal Tudor was under their roof, or anywhere near.

"Howdy," Tudor said shyly.

"How do," Rick replied. Rose said nothing.

Hal seemed embarrassed, as if he knew what they thought of him, as if he sensed their dislike and mistrust.

"Was on my way to Milford Mountain. Stopped in the sutler's yonder. Heard 'im mention you come in for trade a few times. He told me you was up here." He looked down at the ground. "Thought I'd come up and visit." Tudor smiled. "Maybe I could win back some of that pile o' money you won off me before you left."

Rick said, "You never could win when I played. You think your luck's changed now?"

"Well, I've a mind to try'er."

Rick looked at him. "Maybe later."

Slocum wanted to break into his dream and tell White to kill Tudor while he had the chance. There was something very dangerous, and very wrong, about the scout showing up here. Slocum knew that the two were suspicious, but they didn't seem to understand . . . they didn't seem to be paying attention.

Slocum, dreaming, had no mouth; he could not scream a warning. He had no way of communicating with the creatures of his reverie . . . he could only watch. Try as he might, he could only observe. He was powerless to change anything, and powerless to turn away.

John Slocum knew, suddenly, that he would have to watch this dream turn into a nightmare. If he was lucky, he would wake up before it did.

8

The filth and stink of their guest didn't bother Rose or Rick at all—they were used to it. Besides, they smelled themselves. Living, as they did, away from civilization, they never noticed ... much. They were still suspicious. Neither got too close to Hal; both kept a weapon in close reach. Tudor was never left alone—in fact they ate their dinner, which they shared with their guest, outside. None of this was done by plan; the two knew each other so well, and worked so closely, that they didn't have to speak.

Tudor, for his part, did nothing even remotely threatening. He seemed strangely quiet, subdued, ill at ease while they talked.

Rick wondered if Tudor was wishing that he hadn't stopped by to visit. It was as if the man actually realized that his hosts hated, feared, and mistrusted him. Rick was dumbfounded—though he did his damnedest not to show it—at the notion that Hal Tudor had human feelings. Slocum realized that Rick was actually beginning to feel guilty about making a guest feel unwanted, or even about the prospect of hurting his feelings, if it could be said that the man had any. Rick thought that it was real unlikely . . . but Hal looked so sad, almost embarrassed, that it actually became a possibility in his mind.

Slocum didn't believe it for a second. He was picking up warning signals loud and clear. Given what he knew about both Rick and Rose's ability to sense danger, he couldn't imagine that the two of them could be so deaf and blind. Try as he might, however, John couldn't break through into his own dream . . . and it went on.

While they ate, night crept around them, finally embracing them completely. Their rude meal was finished, and what plates and utensils they'd needed out under the stars were cleared and cleaned.

Tudor wiped his mouth with his hair, and began to patiently tie the hair up into two long braids. Nobody said a word. As he was tying the braids with rawhide strips, he sighed, looking deep into the fire. He seemed miles away. Rose looked at her husband quizzically and walked back into the cabin.

Tudor, his huge feet splayed out in front of him, sat before the blazing fire. In the dancing shadows, Rick seemed to see a thousand expressions fleet across the man's face, each only lasting an instant. Rick began to feel sad himself. He was a happy man, with a good life . . . before him sat a man who was beaten down. Rick had seen Tudor driven by blood lust, overjoyed with the chase and the kill of any kind of victim—human or otherwise. He'd thought of Tudor as a rogue animal for so long that he wondered what could possibly have happened to bring out this long buried humanity. *Maybe God is still doing miracles and Hal Tudor has repented of his ways. The Good Lord made the abundance of the earth and the firmament. Maybe He finally put a human heart into one of the most bloodthirsty critters in the mountains.*

Rick stood on the other side of the burning logs, leaning on his rifle, thinking all manner of deep thoughts as he contemplated his guest and watched the stars in the clear night sky. Hal Tudor looked into the fire and sighed again.

In the cabin, Rose sang softly, but in the still of the night, her sweet, husky voice carried out to the two men.

Tudor looked up. "Lucky man."

Rick looked at him. What could he possibly say to the man?

"I am at that. Thanks."

"A body could be happy here."

Rick was touched; he didn't know what the hell to say. "I've got everything I want," he said after a while.

Tudor finally looked him square in the eye. "A fine woman. Money. A goodly cabin. I envy ye, boy."

Rick tried to keep the pride out of his voice. "I built the cabin with my own hands. I earned the money . . . and I guess I was lucky enough to find the right woman."

Tudor shook his head and turned once more to gaze into the fire. "Lucky man."

Tudor sighed and dropped his eyes. Looking absently into the fire for a few minutes, he seemed lost in thought. Rick was more than surprised. He'd never seen the man so thoughtful or subdued. A quick look back toward the cabin told him that Rose, standing in the doorway, shared his puzzlement. The Hal Tudor they'd known was a hard-drinking, sadistic, reckless gambler and killer. This Hal Tudor was like a church mouse—he hadn't blasphemed once, and he'd only once mentioned cards without showing any inclination to actually play. Both Rick and Rose, at the same time, wondered would could possibly have happened to change the old buzzard.

Tudor gazed into the fire for more than a little while, apparently oblivious to his surroundings. Then he got up and began asking Rick questions about the cabin. How long did it take to build? How did he fill the chinks between the logs? Where did he get the wood? He walked around, inspecting closely. Rick followed, at a safe distance, frowning, but he answered all his questions. Tudor stood by the door—he never asked to see the inside—holding a stout piece of firewood. "This wood grow around and about here?" When Rick, carefully standing out of reach, told him that it did, he nodded. "Looks to be good building material." Tudor leaned the wood against the cabin, sat down by the fire, and again lapsed into silence.

Rick kept stealing a glance back at Rose, who kept returning to the doorway, her figure lit by the fireplace behind. Finally she shrugged, and went back to finish her chores in the cabin's shadows.

Tudor eventually looked up. He looked even sadder than before. "Guess I'll make an early start in the morning. Got a camp and some boys workin' with me over at Milford Mountain." He looked at Rick. "Due southwest of here? Ever hear of it?" Rick shook his head. "Oh. Well. It's a good place to light . . . not as nice as this, though. Good enough for the likes of me." He quickly stood and walked around the fire past Rick, gently placing a grimy hand on his host's arm as he passed. "I thank ye for the stew and the company."

Rick looked at him, wide-eyed with surprise. He couldn't for the life of him remember Tudor ever thanking anyone for anything for as long as he'd known the child. As he stared, Tudor walked right past him toward the cabin. Over his shoulder he said, "I'll just say thank 'n good night to the woman."

Rick hardly had time to react. Slocum desperately wanted to warn them not to let the man get between the two of them. But he had no way of saying anything.

Tudor came right up to the portal as Rose came out to see what he wanted; Rick, hurrying to catch up, was just a step behind.

Slocum knew he was too close.

Tudor's left fist came up in a hard jab that clipped right along the side of Rose's head, sending her sprawling and knocking her unconscious. In the same fluid motion, he grabbed the log lying by the doorway in his right hand and swung it around behind him hard . . . Rick walked directly into it.

Only stunned by this blow, Rick tried to blindly

punch out at Tudor, but the man was an experienced fighter and had anticipated the move, stepping back away from the blow and swinging the log two-handed onto the top of Rick's head.

Rick swayed for a moment, trying hard to hold on; strangely, he felt nothing—no pain at all—but he was unable to move his arms or legs. He saw Tudor watching him sway. Suddenly he saw a light so bright that the color was pain. Rick knew that now he and his wife were at Tudor's mercy . . . he never should have dropped his guard. Then he pitched forward onto his face.

Rick came back into consciousness slowly. He could feel himself come up and then start to slide back. He knew that if he let himself go, if he allowed it, he could slip down so far that it would be impossible to ever get back. A part of him wanted that peace; a part of him desired to go on and never return. Rick could feel that wicked, wonderful desire bubble up and begin to take over. It was a great effort to force it down and will himself back. He had to try to save Rose.

At first, he could only hold on by a thread. He felt, at a distance, his hands being tied behind him and his legs roughly tied together. He pushed closer to the surface and felt himself dragged into the cabin.

Slocum, through Rick's uncertain senses, could only make out a jumble of sounds and flashes of vision. Increasingly, Rick became more aware, and Slocum felt Rick's body being tied to the center post of the cabin.

When Rick came back into a stunned sort of consciousness, he finally realized what was being done and attempted to struggle. By that time, it was too late; the post was too sturdy, and Tudor had him securely lashed. Rick watched him turn to Rose.

Rose was moaning and trying to rise when Hal came over and struck her over the ear with a blow strong enough to knock her back down to the dirt, stunned again, but not quite hard enough to knock her out—he wanted her awake and able to feel. He tied her hand and foot.

Using her own knife, he began cutting away her clothes, talking to himself under his breath. Tudor took his time, using rough hands on her and in her while pulling off the clothes. When she was naked, Tudor stood.

Slocum knew what was about to happen now. So did Rick. Pulling and tugging with all his strength only served to make his bonds tighter. Tudor seemed impossibly high to his distorted eye, his head banging against the rafters. He leaned down slowly—so slowly, it seemed to take hours for his face to come close.

"A fine wife, isn't she?" he rasped, his fetid breath and dirt-caked body pressing close. "We wanted her, but she had to have this one, didn't she? Didn't she? Wolf told me how to trick you. He always knows what to do. Didn't think we could play the part so well, eh? Eh?" Kicking Rick hard in the ribs, he laughed as the breath whooshed out of his victim. "We have them now, don't we, Wolf?" Throwing his head back, Tudor howled for all he was worth. "Come, Wolf, come! They're ours now." He howled again and again, in triumph.

Abruptly, he began stalking around the cabin, ripping everything apart, opening chests, flinging garments and utensils around the cabin, which was dimly lit by the fireplace at the back of the room. Tudor was growling and shouting, "We want our money, don't we? Where is it?" Swinging his mad gaze around, he pointed a dirty claw at Rick. "We'll make him talk, Wolf." And again, he tilted his head back and let go a fearsome howl.

This is what it's like to be a mad dog, thought Slocum. This is what I could become. John Slocum's dreaming heart iced over. If he allowed it, his fears could do what the war and Kansas couldn't—his anger would slowly turn him vicious, a rogue animal unfit for human society. He'd be what the good people of the First Calvary Church took him for. It would surely happen . . . the prospect terrified him.

Sweat was pouring off Rick. He felt like he was burning up. He steeled himself, knowing there was nothing he could do for himself or for Rose.

Slocum, after considering and discarding all sorts of plans, had to agree. There was nothing that could be done. Rick and Rose would have to put their energy into dying well. Tudor wasn't going to make it easy.

Rick felt guilty and sorry; guilty for being so careless and letting this madman trap him, and sorry for all the years of joy and happiness that he and Rose and their future family would never have. Bad enough that he would have to watch what Tudor was going to do to Rose, bad enough that he

would have to endure what Tudor was going to put
him through . . . but now he'd never hold his child
or watch it grow; he'd never make love to Rose
again, or see a sunset, or finish the cabin. All that
he and Rose had made would come to nothing. The
life he could have had flashed before his eyes . . .
for a moment he thought he'd cry and scream from
the loss of it. It was a very sad thing and very
unfair. It was much like the Greek tragedies he
used to read when he was a boy.

Slocum felt it, actually, before Rick did. Rick
was preoccupied with his loss, and missed the be-
ginnings of it. To Slocum, it felt like magma bub-
bling up from Rick's center—a flood tide of anger
and resolve gathering speed and momentum, depth
and breadth. It was not hot rage; it was not fury,
unreasoning. Slocum was amazed at the frozen, im-
placable force of will that shot up from the very
center of Rick White.

Everything in Rick was directed at two things
and two things only: watching for the chance to get
Hal Tudor now, and waiting for the chance to get
him even if that meant doing it from beyond the
grave.

Now John Slocum began to suspect that this was
no dream.

Hal Tudor had grown more and more enraged at
not finding any money. Systematically and pain-
stakingly, he was looking through everything, tearing the cabin apart piece by piece. Each time he
looked through a basket of food or a chest full of
clothes and came up empty, he became visibly an-
grier. He then began destroying things without even

looking through them. He interrupted himself only
to howl or discuss something with "Wolf." A few
times he walked over to Rick demanding to know
where the money was buried—he was so positive
that White still had most of the money he thought
of as rightly his. Tudor became even more furious
when it became obvious that punching and kicking
Rick wasn't getting the desired response.

Rose, by now, was conscious. Every time she
made any kind of attempt at rising or moving from
where her tormentor had left her, Tudor would rush
over and smash her with one of his great hands.
There was a trickle of blood coming from one ear,
and a great deal of blood was pouring from her
mouth. She'd spat out two of her teeth, and one of
her eyes was almost closed completely. She never
uttered a word. Rick ached to see her hurt, but he
struggled to hold on to his hatred.

The cabin was a jumble of ripped clothes, broken
pieces of wood, scattered food, and shattered
crockery. Slocum, who'd ridden with Quantrill, and
had witnessed all manner of horror during the War
Between the States, felt sick at heart. He was horrified at the injustice, and at the depraved, crazy
way the life of the Whites was being destroyed. He
had seen this kind of destruction often enough, but
never from inside one of the victims—that made a
powerful difference. Some of what he was feeling
was Rick's outrage and helplessness; some of what
he was feeling came from within his own heart.
John had come to admire and genuinely like these
two people. They had courage and strength, and a
kind of nobility that he wished he possessed. Their

love for each other touched him deeply. He felt that he knew them intimately, and knew that he and they could have been friends.

Tudor stood in the middle of this nightmare jumble, a creature of nightmare himself. His tight buckskins seemed like a layer of black oil, or blood, covering his body. His great feet clutched at the dirt floor like a vulture's claws. The firelight threw angry, moving shadows over everything, and a mad light shone in Tudor's eyes. His hair and beard were so full of grease that they appeared wet in the uncertain light. The front of his pants bulged with an erection. When he threw his arms wide, huge hands grabbing at the air spasmodically, and began to howl, White's home, which had once appeared so sturdy, seemed to shake.

"We want our money now. Don't we, Wolf?"

Tudor stalked over to Rick, grabbed him by the hair, and banged his head against the post. "We want our loot."

Rick said not a word; he only stared. Cool and remote, he seemed to look down on the man, even though he was completely at Tudor's mercy. Rick was challenging Tudor in the only way he could.

Tudor, mad as a hatter, sensed this and understood very clearly. At first, it seemed to anger him, and he rained kicks and blows over Rick's body at a furious pace. Calming a bit, he realized that he might kill his victim too quickly, so he resorted to the sadistic cleverness that Rick had witnessed in him many times before. First, he worked on Rick's legs; holding the ankles with one powerful hand, he pounded the knees with a thick club until he

heard bones crack. Expectantly, he searched Rick's
face, waiting for exclamations of pain, hoping that
he would start to beg. Rick only grunted, and
closed his eyes. In his mind, Rick was taking the
pain, placing it up against his anger and will, knowing it was the only way he could strike back.

He succeeded.

Tudor saw that he wasn't getting the effect he
desired. "Always knew this one was tough. Leave
the woman be for now, Wolf. Back here. There's
plenty of time, plenty of time to enjoy her." Chang-
ing his tactics, he said forcefully, "We ... want ...
the money ... now." With each word, he hit Rick
on the ribs with the club. The blows were two-
handed, with much of the man's great strength behind them. Again, bones snapped.

Rick was sweating profusely, and though the
pain was so great he feared he'd faint, he managed
to keep from screaming ... he knew that if he
started he wouldn't be able to stop. Still, he
couldn't prevent his body—especially the ruined
legs—from twitching and spasming; he couldn't
prevent himself from grunting and grimacing.

These reactions seemed to please Hal Tudor no
end—it meant perhaps that Rick was beginning to
break down. He hoped so. He and Wolf had learned
many valuable lessons from the Indians; it was rare
that a man could take a great deal of pain for a
long period of time before breaking. When he did
break, a man would say or do anything if he
thought that it would lessen or stop the pain ...
there was no end to fun you could have then. Tudor's partner was especially inventive; it was a real

pleasure to see Wolf labor at breaking a body. Sometimes, though, you came across one who wouldn't break, one who got stronger . . . those were a bother . . . took all the fun out of it. Made you feel like you done them a favor. "Oh, Wolf," Tudor said aloud. "I sure hope these two ain't like that."

While Tudor was so busy working on her husband's legs and ribs, Rose had not been idle. Though she'd been kicked time and again, she wasn't afraid to use any opportunity she was given. She wasted little time in worrying about Rick's legs. While Tudor's twisted mind was occupied, she began to move her bruised body toward a broken pot. She thought to cut her bonds, use whatever she could for a weapon, and kill the bastard before he finished the both of them off.

She knew there was little hope, if any. She would have one chance, no more. Tudor was powerful, clever, and he seemed to have eyes in the back of his head. He'd not given her a chance yet. She knew that most men were more careless; most men would have spent too much attention on enjoying their task, or forcing Rick to tell where the money was hidden . . . not that there *was* any money. Rose had the feeling that it really didn't matter that much—the money was an excuse.

Soon he would tire of torturing Rick. He would turn his attention to her. She had to hurry.

Rose worked closer to the shards in small stages, sure that Tudor would turn, sure that he would notice that she'd moved.

The closer she came to her goal, the more she

feared Tudor would turn her way and see what she was doing. Surely she'd attract his attention when she was trying to saw through her bonds. Her back and sides and face were a mass of bruises, and she nearly cried out with every move she made, but still Rose inched closer and closer. Her entire attention was focused on getting her hands free, getting a weapon, and making an end to the ordeal.

Rose didn't want to think about what would have to be done after that . . . would Rick ever be able to walk again? Would they be able to continue their lives as before? Would the baby she carried be able to survive the beating she'd endured? Would Rick be able to survive?

If she failed, there would be no after—they would both be dead, the baby would never be born, there would be no future.

Rick, through a haze of pain that nearly blinded him, had noticed Rose's movements. He knew what she was attempting to do. Though he realized how futile it was, how pathetic their chances, he knew it was the last remaining hope of surviving. He tried to do everything he could to hold Tudor's attention, to get him to forget Rose for just a few minutes. It was just so damn hard to concentrate . . . but he tried.

"Tudor, you foul-smelling bastard, there's no money," he gasped. "I spent it all, like I spent all the money I won from you." It was all he could do to speak without screaming. It was all he could do to forget the pain in his shattered legs, and to stay conscious. The temptation to give in to the enormity of it, to let the pain float him away forever, was terrible. But he knew that if he did that, a frustrated and angry Tudor would turn to Rose. And she would have no chance at all.

Rick began to taunt and insult the man before him, defying him to do something that would really hurt.

Slocum, knowing what Rick was going through, feeling the pain himself, marveled at the amount of punishment the man could absorb without begging or losing consciousness. Slocum was no stranger to pain—he'd endured enough of it in his rough life—but this combination of physical and emotional hurt was more than he'd ever been called upon to take. For John, it was a dream, but still, he felt it take over all his senses. He marveled again at Rick's control. Slocum knew he would never have been able to do what Rick was doing.

Rick's strategy seemed to work—Rose had reached the broken pot, and was beginning to cut through the ropes binding her hands behind her back.

Tudor was in a fury. He'd taken a long, heavy knife, and was slicing deep cuts into Rick's legs, arms, and face. Grunting and cursing, he seemed to have forgotten that Rose existed.

Tudor was realizing that the writhing, bloodied form before him wasn't weakening at all. It bothered him more than a little. This wasn't fun. He'd gotten some reaction out of White for sure—that *could* mean that he was weakening—but it was taking so long. He cast about for a way to speed up the process. "Wolf!" he called as his knife sliced a chunk out of Rick's cheek. "Wolf, think of something."

And Wolf whispered to him. *The woman. Work on the woman now. Let us see if that will bring him where we want him.*

"Yeah. The woman." Wolf always knew what to do. "I'll have that red nigger while he watches." Tudor turned to Rose.

Rose had almost freed herself when Tudor's head turned toward her. She screamed in frustration as he roared and jumped over. Just as he reached her, Rose cut through the rope. She kicked at his groin while reaching for the broken pot behind her.

Tudor held her bound feet with one hand and punched her full in the face with the other. Rose's nose squashed flat against her face, spurting blood in all directions, both eyes blackened at once. He kicked her hard in the stomach. A great noise exploded in her head and she lost her breath. She had failed. Her baby was probably dead already . . . she and Rick would be dead soon. She had failed.

Bleeding from a dozen cuts, the bones in his legs and ribs cracked, Rick knew there was no escaping their fate. Dying, he hoped only to hold on to his resolve. He would not give Tudor satisfaction. He prayed that Rose would have the strength to do the same.

Slocum could hardly believe the man's iron will and endurance.

Through broken teeth and blood, Rick said, "Rose, I'll always love you."

Tudor had just flipped Rose over and tied her hands again. He swung his head around, his grizzled face distorted with anger and fear. "Love!" he shouted. "We'll show you love." Pushing the nearly unconscious woman onto her back, he positioned her so he could watch Rick's face. Untying her feet and kneeling between her legs, squeezing and pulling at her breasts, he opened the front of his pants, exposing his prick. He grasped the shaft in a dirty, bloodstained hand and pushed himself into Rose. She was dry as dust. He expected a cry of pain, he wanted to hear her yell, feel her fight, but she only winced and grunted as he thrust in as far as he could. Tudor looked over to Rick in demonic triumph. "There," he crowed. "That's love, we say."

Rick stared back at him. Through the swollen mask of blood and bruises and cuts, Tudor could plainly make out Rick's icy, unblinking stare. None of this was working out the way it was supposed to. He began to thrust in and out of Rose, howling. He scratched and bit at her breasts and nipples, but she wouldn't cry out. After that first sound when he'd entered her, she'd seemed not to feel a thing. She too stared at him . . . coldly, defiantly.

Tudor couldn't believe it; they always cried or begged or fought—it was best when they did all three. He liked to feel the hurt and helplessness and outrage that leaked out. He began to slap Rose's face; that would keep those eyes off him, but it didn't help. Tudor began to feel himself going soft.

As soon as he stopped slapping her, Rose twisted her head to look at Rick one last time. Unable to speak because of the blood filling her mouth, the look she sent him spoke only of love . . . there was no shame or fear in it.

Rick took his eyes from Tudor. It seemed impossible, but Tudor thought Rick smiled. Startled, Tudor began to slide out of the woman. Wolf whispered in his ear again, and he grew hard . . . Wolf always knew what to do.

Grabbing for his knife, Hal Tudor grabbed Rose by her long hair and pulled upward. He slid the knife hard across her throat, and felt himself come as the hot blood spurted into his face and chest. He rode her thrashing body, laughing.

As soon as Tudor had taken out the knife, Rick knew what was going to happen. For an instant, he thought he would cry out, his will and resolve shattered like his legs. Rick closed his eyes and forced himself to accept even this. When his eyes opened, he was in control again.

Tudor was staring at him steadily; expectantly, waiting for him to explode. As Rick remained impassive, Tudor began to grow afraid. Something was very wrong. There was no money, no satisfaction. Why hadn't they broken? Why hadn't he and Wolf been able to make them grovel? How did they fail?

Rick was staring, staring. He appeared cool and calm. It was as if none of what had happened had been able to reach him. Tudor felt that he had lost. How was it possible?

Hal Tudor felt the red mist of anger rising. He was a man always on the verge of losing control, and he began to lose it now. Wolf was screaming in his ear incoherently; he couldn't make out what

his friend was trying to tell him, and that made him
even madder.

When Rick said, "You lose," Tudor jumped to
his feet, his privates still dangling. His feet grasped
the dirt floor like an ape's. Screaming and raging,
he began to hit himself in the face in frustration.
Wolf was trying to get him to calm down and continue Rick's torture. But Tudor was beyond control;
he threw his body across the cabin and ripped the
knife across Rick's stomach. Blood and entrails
spilled out onto the floor.

Still, Rick only grimaced and grunted, unwilling
to allow his enemy any satisfaction. With a surge
of effort, he fought down the pain and smiled up
at Tudor.

That was the last straw. No longer able to understand Wolf, he just wanted to put an end to the
whole business. There was something wrong here—
something outside his experience. He was beginning to get scared . . . and that was a new emotion
for Hal Tudor.

Slocum watched in horror as Tudor's knife slipped
across Rose's throat. The anger and anguish in
Rick's mind swirled like a storm. Tudor and Rose's
coupling was a terrible imitation of the act of love
and he was disgusted by it. Slocum was awestruck
at how Rick could control himself. The man was
plenty smart, Slocum realized—giving in to emotion was just what Tudor would have wanted. If
Rick had raged and screamed uselessly, Tudor
would have called it entertainment.

Nothing would have changed—perhaps the or-

deal would have been longer, but the outcome
would have been the same. They would have let
Tudor take something precious from them . . . and
he would have laughed in their faces.

Still, weakened by the ordeal and a step away
from death, most people wouldn't have been able
to remain as self-possessed as Rick White; but
then, most people weren't as courageous or as
strong. Few had his iron will. Few had a love as
strong as Rose's to lean on. He drew strength from
her and he remembered her words—that their love
would be good when everything else was bad.

What was most amazing to John Slocum was
that it was true—their love for each other had been
stronger than anything that was done to them. Because they loved so well, nothing could break them
or break them apart. Slocum, though he slept, and
though he *knew* he slept, felt privileged to be a
witness to their life together. He'd heard about love
like that—a few times he even thought he was in
love like that—but he never really believed that it
was possible. Once again, he realized that just
searching for that kind of love, that kind of partner,
with only the hope of finding it, was worth everything. It could make sense out of what he never
could make sense of before. It was enough by itself.

Even though Slocum knew what Tudor would
do after raping and killing Rose, he was unprepared
for the slicing knife, the shock of watching Rick's
body empty blood and organs onto the dirt.

He could feel Rick White begin to fade. He
could sense the start of the slide that would take

him away from this world and into some other.

Then, impossibly, Rick held on.

Tudor's feet had churned up the dirt and gore below Rick into mud, and Tudor swayed, unsteady. Then he stood transfixed—for long minutes, he stared at the man he knew should be dead, unwilling to believe that Rick defied him yet. The knife dropped from Tudor's hands and he backed up a few steps. Lifting his head to the ceiling, he howled, but unlike before, this held no triumph. Now he feared for his own life. He could almost believe that Rick would burst his bonds and drag him off to the hell he thought he'd stopped fearing decades before. He had to make sure that Rick was dead before he left. If he didn't he would spend the rest of his life running.

Fire can stop the demon, Wolf said in his ear. There was even fear in Wolf's voice. Tudor couldn't ever remember Wolf being afraid. But he was right. Wolf always knew what to do.

Rick's eyes seemed to be the only thing in his body that still held life. Those eyes followed Tudor's every movement. He gave the battered body tied to the center post a wide, cautious berth, but he was hypnotized by those eyes.

Their roles seemed to have been reversed. The huge man who'd had Rick at his mercy a short time before, now seemed to be ready to bolt at Rick's slightest move. Never taking his eyes from the man who should have been dead, Tudor moved over to the fireplace and felt behind him. Ignoring singed fingers, he managed to get a flaming stick of wood out onto the floor.

Tudor began to set fire to everything in the back of the cabin. Rick's eyes bored into his unflinchingly. Tearing his gaze away, Tudor made sure that the back of the cabin was burning well.

Slocum felt the hate in Rick. He could truly understand—he too hated Tudor and wanted revenge. He'd already begun suspecting that this was more than a dream. He wondered whether his mind was sleeping or . . . traveling. So much had happened, so much was happening, that he couldn't concentrate. Slocum, forced to watch what had happened to Rick and Rose, had become furious. If he had a purpose in life, it was to prevent himself from becoming an inhuman monster like Hal Tudor.

At one time, it had been tempting—he'd come close to allowing his frustration and self-hatred to drive him to a life dedicated to hurting others. He could have let himself become the kind of man who turned against others and himself. The kind of wandering life he led—drinking, whoring, hiring himself and his gun—had almost taken him in that direction. He'd forgotten to protect himself from that kind of fate. He'd let his mistakes blind him; he'd allowed his own life to hurt him; he'd forgotten he couldn't be perfect. Slocum wanted his life back. He wanted to stop people like Tudor for the rest of his life. John had made plenty of mistakes, but he'd tried not to willingly hurt anyone who hadn't threatened him—he'd even gone out of his way to protect those who were threatened. Slocum realized that he wasn't so damn bad after all.

Next to an animal like Tudor, Slocum was something of an saint.

When he woke, it would be time to get his life back.

He thought of Gerry and the way he was able to use his strength—there was a model for life, there was a man to imitate.

Through Rick's dying spirit and fading vision, Slocum could see that the back of the cabin was burning furiously. Furs, wicker containers, and wooden chests made a good blaze, and it was starting to spread along the rafters. Tongues of blue and yellow spread destruction, their voice a rushing and crackle that would soon be Rick's death.

The burgeoning blaze made a strange light in the room. In the ever-exploding circle of that light, Hal Tudor stood like a mad angel. Every muscle and tendon could be seen as he quivered, his clutching feet turning the once-solid floor into a sticky mess. Looking around, he recognized that he would soon have to leave or become a victim of the flames himself. He'd been so mesmerized by Rick's dying that he'd nearly let the flames trap him.

Slocum saw him shiver and shake his head like a wet dog. It was as if he were coming out of a trance. It looked like he'd regained what passed for his usual control. Tudor seemed confident that the demon Rick White couldn't possibly escape. He wanted to wait patiently to see the flames eat him alive.

Even so, Tudor put as much space as he could between him and the body he'd mutilated. When he reached the door, he turned and spat out, "When me 'n Wolf get back to our mountain, we'll have us a jug and toast you 'n that red bitch in hell." He laughed. "Wolf was right, this'll kill you off. I'll not worry about you followin' me home now."

Rick's eyes, closed these last few minutes, snapped open with such force that Tudor stepped back, banging into the cabin door. With a panicked yelp, he tugged and pulled with all his strength until the hinges were wrenched loose. Flinging the door at Rick, he backed outside. He almost jumped on his horse and rode away, but had to stay . . . just to make sure. Grasping the sides of the opening, he peered in and saw that Rick was still alive. Through a dark mask of blood, surrounded by the flames destroying the home he'd built with his own hands, his eyes shone with life and hate.

Tudor must have found it a fearful picture. Slocum, though, knew that Rick was an inch from death—there wasn't much left of his body or his spirit. John could feel everything the man *did* have focused at Tudor.

Slocum felt himself adding his own feelings to Rick's. They were nearly as forceful and nearly as hateful. Rick seemed to be marking Tudor as judged and sentenced. Slocum wished that it were so. Men like Tudor roamed too freely on the frontier, preying on the innocent and the weak. Tudor could rape and kill and steal his whole life long— and probably had—without the law coming close to him. All the civilization west of the Mississippi couldn't slow Tudor down. All the churches couldn't stop him.

But maybe I can, John Slocum thought.

John could feel Rick's life ebbing, being sucked into some unimaginably deep hole. But though his body died—the last a badly frightened Hal Tudor saw of Rick, his eyes were still open—he resisted being pulled away completely. Rick was, by then, beyond physical pain. He was beyond what is usually thought of as life.

But he wasn't beyond all pain. It was pain that kept him still in this place. There was great pain; that hurt was the loss of his life and the loss of all the things he should have had. It was the unbearable loss of his wife and unborn child that kept him. Rick would not give up the dreams of his life so easily. The force of them lived still. Even now, when there could be no hope of survival, there was hope; even when it was clearly *impossible* to be reunited with Rose, he believed; though he would never be able to strike back at Tudor, Rick searched for a way . . . he would find a way . . . even if he had to live in a world full of memory, he would find a way.

He found John Slocum.

Rick had pushed all his life and energy into a weapon aimed at Hal Tudor. Slocum felt himself being pushed into the point of that weapon thrust toward Tudor's black heart.

Rick White was the gun and John Slocum was the bullet.

As Rick died, John knew, finally, that this was no dream. Slocum opened his eyes.

9

Slocum awoke as the red fingers of dawn were stretching into the dark blue of the night. He came awake immediately, his mind letting go of the long, deep sleep all at once. Sitting up in his bedroll, he listened—except for his own breath, the world was silent. Not a breeze, not a whisper marred that perfect stillness.

Once again, however, he had the feeling that he was being watched, that there was something just at the edge of his vision.

There was.

Three owls sat in the rafters of the burnt-out cabin. As he looked, they slowly spread their great wings, lifted, and flew away into the night.

Life was very, very strange.

John Slocum had come up onto this mountain a man dead in heart and soul. When he laid his head down in this place of broken hope, he had dreamed of a man dead in all *but* heart and soul. He felt that Rick had asked him to do a job. Rick was hiring

him to find and kill Hal Tudor. But what would be
his pay? Slocum had a very real feeling that a reward was being offered—but what was it?

Could it be the money that Tudor had coveted?
No. Rick had spent it as soon as it was won. Whatever it was, did Slocum want the job? Did he want
to go through all the trouble of finding Tudor and
then trying to kill him? Slocum wasn't even sure
that he *could* do that after everything that had happened in the past few months.

Kill Hal Tudor. *Even in my prime I don't know
that I could have taken the man on. And he's got
more men with him now.*

Standing and walking out into the clearing, Slocum wondered if his brain was addled. Maybe this
was all manufactured by his crazy mind. It was too
crazy to be true. In the cold dawn, it seemed too
crazy, too unreal.

But Slocum knew that it was all true, all of it.
He *knew* that he'd been shown actual events, and
that somehow, some way, Rick White wanted him
to kill Hal Tudor. Hell, Slocum wanted to himself.

Did he have the courage? Did he still possess the
skill? How the hell was he going to find the man
after all this time?

Slocum's mind was full of questions—he didn't
have answers for any of them right now.

Why was he bothering with all this anyway?
Again he thought this was a crazy, stupid notion—
a figment of his tortured mind; maybe even the
result of some bad food. That was it—spoiled food
caused crazy nightmares. He must be loco to believe that there were ghosts trying to talk him into

killing someone who probably didn't even exist.

John looked around at the cabin and listened hard to the still silence on the mountain. *Even if this is all true, it's none of my affair.* It was all so crazy. *Why don't I just forget about it and move on? Just forget about it all?*

And that was just what he started to do. He quickly collected his belongings, loaded up, and made ready to leave. His mind was empty, the sun was coming up. He mounted.

And he sat there. Slocum looked at what was left of the cabin; he looked around at the clearing and the trees and the scrub already beginning the inexorable process of erasing everything that had been done here. His mind flooded with Rick White's memories. They were as clear as any he had.

Slocum thought about the past few months and what his life had been like—how he'd hated himself, hated living.

What would the future be like if I left this place and never looked back? It would, he knew, be like the past, *only worse.* He didn't think he'd be able to stand that.

During the dream, or whatever it was, Slocum remembered thinking that he could become like Tudor. That could happen—as sure as the sun comes up, that could happen to him. Maybe he'd already gotten his reward. *Maybe I owe Rick for the dream; maybe killing Tudor is my way of paying Rick back for everything he's done for me.*

Slocum hated Tudor—he'd be doing himself a favor by killing the bastard. Slocum hated what he'd done to Rick and Rose—hell, he'd taken a bullet from Quantrill trying to stop a man like Tudor. He hated what Tudor had done even more because it was done to *him* too. He hated it because he was more afraid of becoming like Hal Tudor than anything else he could think of.

Lord above. If I can do this, there ain't nothin I couldn't do. If I could do this, I could look myself in the mirror without bein' afraid of what I might find, or what I'd turned into.

Slocum always thought of himself as the kind of man who looked after his friends, the kind of man who didn't let his friends down. He surely thought of the Whites as his friends now. *I was always the kind of man who wasn't afraid to take on someone like Tudor if I had to.*

Slocum used to be the kind of man who could survive in a hard and dangerous world—he wanted to be that kind of man again.

Sitting on his horse, surrounded by the growing brightness of day, Slocum thought. *Shit! I'm going to do it.* He smiled and shook his head. *It's my medicine. There ain't no one else for the job.*

Slocum thought about the things Tudor must have done, and all the things that he would do. All the things he would never be brought to justice for. Tudor was too tough, too clever, too loco. There just wasn't enough law in the whole territory to bring him down. All the prayers west of the Mississippi couldn't stop Hal Tudor.

But I can.

Now John Slocum could leave. He started back down the mountain, actually happy for the first time in months. As he moved through the trees and further and further from the cabin, he began to hear birdsong; in the distance, he could see deer. It made him glad. For the first time in too long, he felt like he was whole again. Something had been cleaned from him, some awful poison. He was glad to be back in the world. Horrible as it could be, he was glad to be back.

It was a funny world, all right. He'd come here sick at heart over the killing of a man. Now he was leaving a haunted camp glad to be on the trail of killing another. There was just no accounting for the things that happened; there was just no sense in asking sometimes. Most of the time you just had to do what had to be done, and be glad you were alive to do it.

When he thought about Cahill this morning, he regretted what had happened—he was sorry for Cahill's boy—but he knew it *was* an accident. It wasn't the way he'd wanted it to happen, and he'd move heaven and earth to stop it from happening again if he could. But there was no taking it back. A man did his best to stay alive—that was first; he did his best not to hurt anyone else; he did his best to enjoy the good things of life and destroy the poison in the world. It was so clear all of a sudden. It made sense. Slocum couldn't wait to get through all this and get back to talk to Gerry. *Now that I've turned into one of them philosophers, I might be able to give him a little advice.*

Slocum laughed out loud, and looked to the southwest.

•   •   •

He came down from the mountain thinking hard on how to find Hal Tudor—this was a mighty cold trail to follow. He no longer worried about whether he could find him, or whether he should. Slocum was just going to do it.

Something had changed. He'd gotten back some of what he'd lost, that was clear, but he'd gained something too. Maybe it was a new kind of confidence; perhaps it was a different sense of purpose than the one he'd had before. Maybe the ordeal he'd put himself through had made a tougher man out of him. He thought a lot about this as he rode. But as deep as Slocum pondered, he didn't seem to come up with much of an answer. One thing he did know—he was different.

As he rode, he was also alert; sharper than he'd been in a long, long time. He was happier, more joyful. *Guess I learned something from Rick and Rose.*

Milford Mountain lay somewhere to the southwest, and it was there that he would find Hal Tudor—if he was to find him at all. He figured on the simplest plan available—he'd ride in that direction and ask. He'd ask anyone and everyone about the mountain and about Hal Tudor. The mountain might be a little hard to find—after all, one mountain is pretty much like another. Hal Tudor . . . once you've seen him, you're not likely to forget it.

The trick would be finding Tudor without him finding out that some stranger was asking around about him. If Tudor tumbled to the fact that a man was looking for him, it would be harder than impossible to bring him down. Slocum's best weapon was going to be surprise.

The trick after that would be spying on his camp and getting the lay of the land without being discovered. That was going to be pretty difficult; Tudor was an experienced tracker and scout himself. Rick remembered Tudor as a very dangerous man— one who knew how to protect himself in Indian country, one who knew how to outwit Indians at the game they'd invented.

The trick after that would be approaching the camp without getting killed, or worse yet, captured. Slocum had seen and felt—first-hand—what Tudor and Wolf were capable of; the men who would be with him weren't likely to be much friendlier. One thing, though. They couldn't be any worse. John Slocum couldn't think of a harder opponent than Tudor. Next to Hal, anyone else was likely to be easy.

The trick after that would be killing Tudor and staying alive. It might be some easier if Slocum was willing to give up his life to get Tudor, but right now John was beginning to enjoy being in the world again. He wanted to stay around a bit yet.

Slocum wondered if he were magician enough to pull that many rabbits out of his hat. Well, he figured, the first trick might not be too hard, the second was difficult, the third was a real problem, and the fourth was probably impossible. It would be a miracle if he survived this. *Yeah, but if I do, well, then, I can just start believing in miracles. Certainly gives me something to work up to.*

The prospect of facing Tudor had him plenty

worried. Slocum considered this a very healthy sign. He was going to have to puzzle out a way to shift the odds in his favor . . . they were going to have be shifted a long way. John didn't know how he was going to do that yet. He was surprised at his confidence. He really shouldn't have any; didn't have too many reasons to feel so good about this— after all, he was probably going to die.

Fact was, Slocum did have confidence in his fighting ability—with any kind of weapons. John knew he was fast, strong, smart, experienced . . . if he kept up his confidence, got sharp again, and used his brain, why, he might be able to work himself up to having one chance in hell.

Slocum laughed.

As the days wore on, Slocum began to feel better and better. A part of him was expecting to slide back. But he just kept on. He slept well—with no dreams that he could remember, thank heaven. He ate plenty of good, fresh red meat to build up his body and strengthen his blood. He moved slowly, hunting for food; then once he'd made a kill, he camped. He ate what he killed, stayed a few days, then left. It was a waste of game, he knew, but first things first—he had to get his strength back. He practiced shooting, stalking, and moving quietly. He bathed whenever he could—staying clean seemed to make him feel better; it relaxed him. In the course of a few weeks, he moved slowly south and a little west down out of the mountains and to the edge of the desert.

Up to now he'd actually been avoiding people,

choosing to wait a bit before having to deal with them. He preferred to use the time to think. Around the time he needed to stock up on supplies—he was running low on ammunition for the pistol and the rifle—he also thought he'd like to talk to a human being again. He sat one night, looking at the stars, and realized that it had been weeks since he'd talked to another person. He felt remote, like the sky-spanning dots of light that held such fascination for him; he didn't want to be that remote. Except for his dream—*Jesus! does that count?*—he'd only seen a few people in all that time, and those from a distance.

John had in mind to find a town and begin asking around about his quarry. He'd ask a few questions and maybe find out if he could still talk like a white man after all this time. Just might feel good to pass the time with someone for a little bit.

John Slocum was not the kind of man who needed much company usually; usually he'd rather make do with his own company just fine. These days, however . . . These days, much had happened to him and he'd been brought lower even than when he was in Kansas. A little company besides his horse and his own thoughts might be a welcome change for a little bit.

Slocum angled back and forth looking for a road, reasoning that a road would have to go somewhere from somewhere else. When he did find one, it looked sufficiently well traveled, and he followed it. The country it passed through quickly got drier and there were fewer trees. Soon there were none at all.

He traveled the better part of a day without passing a house or another person. The road, however, seemed to show heavy traffic.

Topping a small rise, he saw a town about a mile below him, ringed round by low hills and a sorry-looking lake.

There were about five shacks ranged along one side of the road. The lake was behind the houses and Slocum didn't see any boats on the surface. A couple of people were visible around one of the structures, and Slocum found himself happy at the sight.

He rode along, wondering at the difference between how he'd felt a month ago and how he felt now. This was no bustling metropolis—he was unlikely to find much of interest here—he would be lucky if he picked up any information at all.

I guess any kind of conversation would be welcome.

A disheveled little man was standing in front of the first building Slocum passed. Obviously, the man had seen him coming and waited to speak to John as he rode in. *Must be the welcoming committee.* Looking down at him, Slocum was amused by the battered bowler hat, at least one size too big, sitting on the back of the man's head. Wisps of curly gray hair stuck out at all angles from underneath the hat, and he had his thumbs hooked into a gaudy vest that had seen better days . . . much better days. His brogans were much too big for his feet and the toes pointed up.

The man watched with a big grin on his face as Slocum approached, as if the sight of a stranger was the best thing that had ever happened to him.

Slocum thought that the hat and vest might have been a pretty fancy number at one time. Now, however, both had seen a lot of wear—the hat was stained and dented in the oddest places, and had chunks taken out of the stingy brim; the vest had one huge yellow stain down the front and was worn and frayed all along the bottom.

Slocum stopped his horse as he rode up to the man, touched the brim of his hat, and said, "Howdy," in his friendliest voice.

The man's grin doubled, if that were possible. Slocum could see some badly stained teeth. "Hey, mister. What brings you here? Nice day, ain't it? Bet you're hot—it's always hot around here even though we got us a real lake over yonder. Where you from? Where you goin'?"

John sat back and looked down at the little bird now grinning up at him again. "Just passin' through," he said quietly. "What's the name of this town?" Slocum motioned with his hand. He made sure to smile.

"Where you headed, mister? You plannin' to stay awhile? Nobody stays here, everbody just rides on through, don't even stop for a drink. Sure would be somethin' if you decided to stay, why don't you? You probably got business somewhere's else, aintcha? What business you in?"

Slocum blinked a couple of times, stunned. This little man was trying to get a lot of conversation in as quickly as he could—maybe he was worried that his visitor would disappear before he could get it all out. *Probably a good idea too*. John had already decided to ride on, but he thought he might try to get some information out of this welcoming committee.

All right. Let's try again.

"Not plannin' to stay anywhere. Just roamin' around seein' the elephant. What's the name of this place anyway?" Slocum somehow didn't think he was going to get a straight answer.

Still grinning mindlessly, the man started up again. "Elephant? Ain't no elephants around here. What's an elephant? What's your name? You got a name, mister? Everbody's got a name. Everbody calls me Allie, but that ain't my name. My daddy used to say, 'What's in a name?' all the time. I never could figure out what he was talkin' about. What d'you think he meant? Where'd you come from, mister? Had to be more interestin' than this dumb place. Whyn't you get on down and have a drink, must be hot."

Slocum leaned back in the saddle a little overcome by the rapid-fire questions. He was sure now that he'd learn nothing from this one. He was sure also that he wasn't going to join him in a drink either—he might never get free. *Jee-zus. So much for a little pleasant conversation.*

John figured himself for a damn fool, but he was going to give it one more try—just out of curiosity. As slow as he could manage spacing each of the words, he said, "What . . . is . . . the . . . name . . . of . . . this . . . town?"

It didn't do any good.

"Why you talkin' so slow, mister? You tired? I get tired and I don't even do much. My daddy used to say I could get tired sleepin'. He'd say, 'You could tire yourself out sleepin', boy.' Just like that. We'd all laugh and laugh. Daddy's dead now—got drunk, stubbed his toe, an' we had the biggest wake and funeral, it was great—"

"Hold it," Slocum said. He just couldn't hold himself back. "Your daddy died by stubbing his toe?"

"Naw. You're funny, mister. Daddy fell in the lake and drowned *after* he stubbed his toe. We was sorry to see him go, he was a caution an' . . ."

Slocum sighed and ran his hand over his face. He let the fool run on. Looking around at the town—whatever it was called, he didn't give a shit now—he saw five weather-beaten buildings, lots of what appeared to be rusted mining machinery, and a few mules. No other people seemd to be about. *Probably inside out of the heat.* It was hot, Slocum realized. Damn hot. He took off his hat, and wiped his head with a handkerchief. Maybe he should get down and check around, see if someone could tell him where the hell he was. Maybe somebody in this godforsaken place had heard of Milford Mountain.

Setting his hat back on his head, he guessed that if he did get down, he'd have a shadow following him—a shadow that never stopped asking questions. Slocum wasn't sure that he was up to it. It was best to just go on.

". . . and Daddy was going to build a *boat,* that's why he walked up to the lake and died—I tol' you about that—so Cousin Jimmy was over in the out-house with a powerful bad stomach an'—"

"Well, pardner," Slocum said absently, "I guess I'll just be movin' on. I got a mountain to find." He touched spurs lightly to his mount's sides and began to move away. The man followed him down the street.

"A mountain, huh? Which mountain you lookin' for? Why you lookin for a mountain? I like mountains. They're high. You like mountains, mister? I bet there's lots of mountains, more'n I can count, I bet, though I can't count so high. I never did learn to calculate so good, but it wasn't my fault 'cause we didn't have no school. Momma tried to teach me, but she said I didn't learn so well. She said, 'Why don't you try to learn, you're just like . . .'"

The voice droned on in the heat, and even seemed to increase in speed as Slocum urged his horse into a trot. Help! Slocum thought.

The man was panting as he ran alongside the horse ". . . an' Cousin Ephraim let me ride on the mail wagon all the way to Coty 'cause he felt sorry for me after Daddy died an' he named every mountain we passed an' I remember 'em all, there was Scooley's Mountain an' White Mountain an' Scandia Mountain an' Milfert's Mountain an' Cat's Peak an' Jenny's Mountain an'—"

Slocum reined up fast. "Hold it," he said.

The little man ran on a bit before stopping and turning around. "You gonna say something funny again, mister?"

Slocum tipped his hat back. "That depends. Did you say Milfert's Mountain? or Milford Mountain?" He was sure to smile nice and friendly—didn't want to scare the man.

"I don't know, mister. I say a lot of things. I like to talk. Momma used to say, 'I never seen nobody talk the way you do.' Just like that. Momma died of the fever. I was little an'—"

Slocum put up both of his hands. "Hold it," he said again. "I can see that this is going to take some time. Where can we get a drink?"

An hour later, Slocum stumbled out of the only saloon in town—a low-ceilinged, rickety shack with a warped plank for a bar. His head swam, and not from spirits either. He'd gotten a good idea where Milford Mountain was—though he still didn't know the name of the town he was in.

He did learn that Milford Mountain was about a day's ride west along the road to Coty—which, for some ungodly reason, was known as the Plank Road—and then nearly a day's ride due north of the road. The mountain was supposedly easy to spot; it rose some five thousand feet high, and stood alone on the desert floor. The top was flat, as if the tip had been sawed off, and was covered by the ruins of an ancient Indian city. No one knew which Indians had built it. No one had mentioned Hal Tudor either. Slocum had decided against asking about him. The bartender was too suspicious, it just didn't feel right . . . whatever it was, Slocum counted himself lucky to have found out the location of the hideout so quickly. Better not to ask for too much from one source. Slocum was going to have to ask around and see what he could learn somewhere else.

Mounting up, Slocum spied the bartender out of

the corner of his eye—he hadn't gotten his name either. The man was squinting at him from the doorway of the shack that passed for a saloon in this desolate excuse for a town. The man's eyes were clenched so hard they were almost closed. John didn't like being watched so hard; it made him more than a little nervous. Touching the brim of his hat politely, he turned his mount and headed west along the Plank Road.

Moving slowly, taking in the scenery—which wasn't much to look at—as if he didn't have a care in the world, he rode through the heat and the dust.

About five miles out, after making sure he wasn't followed, John doubled back a bit. Picking a hill with good concealment, he hobbled the horse, found a place to watch the road, and settled down. *Let's see if anyone decided to follow me.*

He'd relearned a lesson in patience from Rick. If anyone was going to warn Tudor, or follow the stranger asking questions, they'd probably use this road. Slocum wanted to know if they did.

He would wait patiently. Because he was taking on an animal like Hal Tudor, it was better to make sure there were no surprises. Tudor would be difficult enough without surprises.

It was the bartender that had decided him on this course of action. It was something in the way he moved . . . something in the way he'd acted when he saw Slocum that had gotten those hackles up.

Slocum had walked into the low-ceilinged, cramped room and waited a few seconds for his eyes to adjust from the bright sunlight outside to the dim light. The saloon was empty except for the bartender. He sat on a pile of sacks, squinting at the two men as they entered. The little man didn't say anything to him. The bar was a plank held up by two battered sawhorses. Two long shelves behind held a score of dusty bottles and glasses. The man behind the plank was a dark Mexican, and he didn't seem very happy to have a couple of customers.

Maybe he's had enough of the little man with me here.

John couldn't blame him. His companion was simple and harmless—but he truly didn't know when the hell to shut up. A man could get real tired of him real fast. Even now, he'd begun chattering away about some damn thing. Slocum ignored him. The bartender didn't even look his way.

Slocum looked at the barman; he was dark and heavyset, though short. His cheekbones and eyes and chin were strangely pointed—as if they'd been sharpened. His nose, though, was mashed down to one side, flat. He seemed to have a perpetual scowl, and a perpetual squint.

John did his level best to appear friendly. He smiled. "Two whiskeys, please." He turned to his new friend. "You do drink whiskey, don't you?"

"Sure I drink, mister. I like to drink, makes everything look better. My daddy taught me how to drink. He said. . . ."

Slocum let him run on, and held up two fingers. He said please again too.

The bartender didn't acknowledge either of them. He wiped his hands on a dirty apron and took down a bottle without a label and two glasses.

When they were put on the plank, he squinted at Slocum. The man's knuckles and fingers were scarred, swollen, and misshapen. His ears looked like puffed-up flowers.

A bare-knuckle fighter, Slocum thought.

John could feel anger flowing off the man in front of him. He was staring boldly, waiting for Slocum to complain, hatred radiating from his thick body like heat.

Slocum felt pretty damned uncomfortable. *What the hell's going on here?* He decided he would ignore it for as long as he could. He'd inquire about the mountain, but not about Tudor.

Though the little man was still jabbering away, Slocum continued to ignore him and spoke directly to the bartender. "Little fella here tells me that a place called Milford Mountain ain't too far away. How far is it?"

The bartender's mustache twitched, and Slocum thought that he was about to speak, but he remained silent. Maybe he was waiting for Slocum to say more. John almost asked about Tudor. He almost asked about his old friend Hal Tudor, the scout. Slocum almost made up a good story to go with the request. Almost.

John wasn't too sure about what it was that stopped him, but he decided to just let it be. He didn't mention Tudor's name, didn't explain why he was asking about the mountain, or give his name or anything. He waited for the bartender to answer.

The little man was still yammering away like there was nothing else going on. The fact that he was being ignored so obviously didn't seem to faze him in the least. Slocum was beginning to get used to him. He found it easier to block him out.

Slocum tried to appear casual and friendly, but he was concentrating on his battle of wills with the bartender. There was a shotgun—well-oiled and shining in contrast to the rest of the place—leaning against the wall just under the shelves. And there was a bulge of something—a knife?—under the bartender's apron. The tension between the two men was obvious. Slocum hoped that it wasn't going to turn ugly—he was hoping to save his energy for the big battle that he knew was yet to come.

Slocum took his eyes away and sipped at his drink, still trying to appear casual. He looked around. The room was a mess—there was a table and chair in a corner, caked with dust; nobody had sat there in a while. The floor was strewn with broken bottles, unbroken glasses, yellowed newspapers, pieces of wood, and all manner of debris; John had trouble making it all out in the uncertain light even after his eyes had grown used to the dimness.

It was a very strange scene; the little man was jabbering away, the bartender was scowling and squinting, twitching his mustache from side to side, and Slocum stood there smiling like a ninny, waiting.

The drink was surprisingly good. Whatever else this place was, it had a tasty stock of spirits. Slocum finished his drink, told his companion to drink up and get ready for another—that sure shut him up for a minute—and asked for two more.

After the second was finished, the little man actually shut up—for the first time since they'd met. He just leaned up against the wall and closed his eyes. He never said another word.

Slocum was just beginning to wonder where all this was going to end up when the bartender began to talk about Milford Mountain. Slocum had no idea what had happened—one minute it looked like he was about to get into a fight, and the next minute, everything was peaceful.

I couldn't have imagined this.

Slocum thanked the man behind the bar and left. The little man seemed to be asleep on his feet. Slocum never saw him again.

Peculiar place, he thought as he walked out.

He watched the town for a few hours. No one left. No one passed.

He decided that it was safe to continue.

Damned strange. Wonder what that place is called.

Riding along the Plank Road, he figured he should be close after a day's ride—if the bartender was telling the truth. Didn't seem to be any reason why he should be telling the truth actually. Slocum more than half expected that he'd been lied to. If his luck was really bad, he was riding into some kind of a trap, or at least a wild-goose chase.

Well, after all this time, a few more days on the road aren't going to make much of a difference. I'll just keep on looking until I get it right. Almost seems too damn easy this way anyway. Like it was meant to happen.

It was an arid landscape he was riding through. Off to either side, red and brown hills stood up tall, and in between, the land was terribly cracked and fissured. It was inhospitable and had the feel of emptiness—an old, long-established emptiness. It had an unfriendly feel too. Didn't seem that the land would accept a man's hand very easily or happily. *Just the kind of territory that Tudor would feel at home in.*

Except for the road, there wasn't a human sign anywhere. Slocum thought that he might as well have been traveling on the moon, or some such place: a place where humans had never been, and never would be either.

There was no wind, not a breeze; just the heat and the dirty hills. There was Slocum and his horse and sweat . . . the sweat dripped off him. His horse plodded listlessly, John swayed listlessly . . . and both horse and rider felt their energy drain.

The more he rode, however, the more he believed that he'd been told the truth. He could *feel* Tudor. This was his kind of place. This was the kind of country that drained a man, made him careless, weakened him. Hal Tudor would count that as an advantage. Slocum's sixth sense told him that he was on the right trail.

He resolved to stay alert, keep his wits about him. He was surprised at how easy that was now. A part of Slocum watched and smelled and heard and felt all around as he rode. Another part thought and pondered and weighed.

Slocum didn't torture himself this time out. He had a lot on his mind. Tomorrow, sometime,

he might be able to see Milford Mountain—
something that distinctive might be visible in
this dry air. He decided that he'd ride past, go
on to Coty, and see if he couldn't learn something about Tudor.

Maybe the people over in Coty were a little more
normal than those in the nameless town he'd just
left. Maybe he'd be able to talk to people in Coty.
He'd like that: to have a drink and talk about horses
and gossip and pass the time of day. It would be a
nice feeling.

Maybe he could find out if Tudor had been seen
in the area. It was a strong possibility that Tudor
had moved on. *Hell. He could be dead by now*.

John hoped that wasn't true—this was his only
lead on the man. He had no idea what he'd do if
he found out that Tudor had pulled up stakes and
headed out to anywhere else. If that were true, there
was little chance that Slocum would be able to hunt
him down.

It was a big country, and it could swallow a man
easily.

Slocum didn't think that was true either. He expected to find Hal Tudor, and the other men, just
where he was told they were going to be.

Okay. Say they are there. What then?

How was he going to get close to them? And
once he did manage to get among them, how was
he going to kill them and still ride off in one piece?

These thoughts took a lot of Slocum's attention.
When the sun began to set, he was still deep into
them, and he still hadn't come up with anything.

How in hell am I going to even up these awful odds?

He considered and rejected many ideas. All he knew was that he was going to try it. Come what may.

He made his camp just before sunset. With the sun gone, it wasn't long before the sun's heat disappeared and the desert cooled off. Soon it was downright cold. Slocum didn't want to build a fire—too easy to see—so he spent the night wrapped in blankets, looking at the stars.

He'd always been fascinated by the night sky; fascinated and even a little comforted. It was the grandest show to be had, and the most mysterious. It calmed his mind and his soul . . . he'd always done his best thinking at night.

He slept. He didn't dream.

During the night, he woke to the long, low, mournful howling of a lone wolf.

Usually, that sound affected him the way it had affected most humans for millennia. Usually, it set his short hairs standing straight, his teeth to grinding, and his hands gripping for the nearest weapon. Tonight, though, it sounded like some strange, ancient musical message. It was a song of Spirit, a tale of Power. Slocum felt that he was a part of it in some way.

The wolf was nearby, his voice deep, like a baritone, and moving slowly up the scale. The howls were a few seconds long, with hardly a breath, it seemed, in between. Soon, the one wolf was joined by the pack in a chorus rising to a scream. Slocum could hear everything very clearly, so clearly that he could even hear the yipping and high-pitched voices of pups underneath it all.

The only time Slocum had heard its equal was during the war when Pickett's twelve thousand men screamed the Rebel yell in the tall grass on their way up Cemetery Ridge. Their mad, foolish noise filled the lush Pennsylvania countryside until they were drowned out by the Yankee cannons, by the muskets and the whistle of minié balls, by the screams of wounded men . . . Slocum's brother died in that grass. These wolves affected Slocum in the same way.

Suddenly, in the distance, another wolf began howling in answer, his voice also starting out low and rising. This wolf's howls were longer—Slocum counted twelve seconds on one. This wolf was then joined by his pack, and the two groups of wolves filled the moonlit night with their dreaming songs. Their voices were inhuman, and old beyond measure, and Slocum found them familiar.

When a third and a fourth pack began howling, Slocum realized that he was in the center of the groups. By then, the song was running in his blood.

The wailing pandemonium was sent up into the night in huge sweeping spirals of sound aimed at the moon and at the heart of the world.

It was as if huge portals had opened. The stars, uncounted legions of them, blazed overhead, the wolves' cries directed at one after the other of them. The screaming howls lost their mournfulness and became a kind of link between the animals of hot blood, the unconscious molten-hearted world they inhabited, and the spinning, unimaginably alien worlds of infinity.

The night, the cold, the stars, and especially the unceasing, undulating voices of the wolves, filled Slocum completely—he couldn't have said or thought his own name. He lifted his head and threw his own howls into the darkness. Hal Tudor's mad howling was a pathetic, demented imitation of this—the way his rape of Rose White was a horrible imitation of lovemaking.

John Slocum didn't think it was strange to fling wordless questions, mindless rage, fearful agony, and barrierless joy into the darkness between the stars. He shivered and trembled and beat his hands against the earth until his palms and arms ached.

How long it went on, he didn't know.

One by one, the wolves dropped off from their songs; finally, Slocum was exhausted. The night was silent again.

Before Slocum fell into the deepest, most satisfying sleep he'd ever known, he realized that the wolves had told him what to do. But he just couldn't understand. If only he could translate. If only he could decipher the sign, he would know the way to defeat Tudor.

He slept.

In the morning he set out again, refreshed, along the Plank Road. At mid-morning, almost due north, he finally did catch a glimpse of Milford Mountain off in the distance. Just as he was told. Slocum had the good sense to be surprised. He'd really not expected the mountain to be there.

The heat was beginning to become intense, and Slocum knew that he should try to learn what he could in Coty before going on to confront Tudor. He wanted to get it all over with quickly, but he decided to curb his impatience.

He rode on toward Coty.

He was looking forward to a cold beer and the sound of human voices. In Coty, he could find that. And maybe a word or two about Hal Tudor. If the man was up there on Milford Mountain, he would have to go someplace for supplies; if not in Coty, then someplace to the north or northeast. Slocum would ring the mountain until he found out. It was likely, however, that Coty—less than two days' ride southwest of his hideout—was a place that got a good deal of Tudor's business.

Slocum had no doubts about one thing—if Tudor ever visited, he would be remembered.

Looking at the rock rising in the shimmering air, Slocum could feel Tudor's presence. He could smell evil and blood lust on the wind. Rick had pointed him at the right place. Slocum knew he'd found the bastard—he had only to confirm it.

In his mind's eye, he could see just what would happen. He'd ride into Coty, he'd stop and drink at the first saloon he came to; there he would meet someone, get to talking, and he'd mention Tudor's name, and the man would know him by sight and reputation. Slocum would be warned to stay away from him. . . .

John almost felt like he didn't have to go on.

If it wasn't for the fact that he really needed a cold beer and another voice, he probably would go into those hills east of the mountain and wait to see what he would see. He was that sure he'd found the place.

As he rode on, he wondered again what it was the wolves had tried to say to him the night before.

10

Riding into Coty, John Slocum felt like a school-boy at Christmas—he actually howdied a few of the people he passed in the dusty street. He came riding into the little place around dinnertime, just after sundown. The yellow lights in the homes where families gathered to share a meal, and the bright lights of stores spilling out into the street, filled his heart with a kind of joy he hadn't felt in a long, long time.

He couldn't wait to get back to Golden and tell Gerry about all of this. Maybe that philosopher's wisdom of his could help Slocum to understand some of what had been going on.

Right now all I got is questions—just like always.

If that was so, then why did he feel so damn happy?

Coty really wasn't much of a place. It certainly was more of a town than that strange little collection of shacks by the lake, but it wasn't as big as

Golden or Muffresboro. So little can make up joy in a man's mind when he needs companionship that even a poor, rude place like Coty could make John's heart happy.

The lights from the buildings in the closing dark, the people riding and walking back and forth, and especially the voices coming from the buildings pleased him no end. Slocum rode down the town's one long street looking around with a great idiot grin on his face, and he didn't care what people thought of him. Though he was hungry for food, talk was what he craved most—and the best place for that was a saloon.

Stopping at the first he came upon, Slocum looped the reins around a hitching rail and practically ran into a room filled with smoke and the loud, raucous noise of men talking and arguing and laughing.

There were tables full of cardplayers, serious and intent, surrounded by circles of onlookers—just as serious and intent. The talk there was minimal— only the occasional necessary word, a grunt of pleasure, derision, or admiration. Other tables were filled with men playing at cards much less seriously—there the talk was loud and more the point than gambling.

Other tables were awash with political debate. Fists were shoved into faces, boots stomped away in passion and answered just as passionately. Words flew, men grasped each other's arms.

The bar was lined with drinkers in groups of twos and threes deep in discussion. Their eyes were alight with alcohol, their voices strained and fervid, the gestures sharp. No one seemed to be alone, no one seemd unengaged . . . except for Slocum. The lights were bright and all noises—scraping chairs, clinking glasses, shouting voices—seemed louder than they should be.

Slocum loved it all.

Most of the men seemed to be miners or men who worked for the mines in one way or another, and there didn't seem to be any women around.

From just inside the doorway, Slocum looked benignly on this chaos, savoring it before joining in. Then he bellied right up to the bar and shouted for a beer from one of the bustling, harried bartenders.

As he was handed the glass, Slocum shouted over the din, "Jesus! You're doin' some business tonight. Is it always like this?"

The young man serving drinks slid a full beer mug down the polished, wet wood and replied, "Naw. Big doin's. The three Nakes brothers all got married at the same time today. Everybody from the mine come to town for the wedding. They been celebrating all day."

Slocum, sipping the cold brew, nodded, then looked around. "They gone, are they? I don't see no brides or grooms around."

"Yeah. Left early." The bartender—Slocum thought he looked barely old enough to drink—raised and lowered his eyebrows a couple of times and said, "Woo-woo."

Slocum laughed and said, "Woo-woo," right back, and watched as the young man hurried down to fill more glasses. What a delightful boy, he thought. It's a pleasure to talk to him.

Turning his back to the bar and hooking a boot heel over the polished brass rail, Slocum drank the rest of his beer and watched the room. He was vastly entertained by everything he saw and heard. *Big difference from the last couple of saloons I visited.* John finished his beer and went to the free food table, made himself a sandwich, and gulped it down. He *was* hungry. His body satisfied for the time being, Slocum returned to his place at the bar and got another drink.

People were coming in and leaving all the time, rushing up and calling for a drink, then running off to speak with friends. One of these, a medium-sized older gent with a short gray fringe of hair and an elaborate handlebar mustache, tripped and spilled half his glass of whiskey over Slocum's shirt.

"Oh, damn! Sorry, stranger. And that was the best drink I ever had too."

Both men laughed.

"This is too much fun for an old geezer like me. I'll have those clothes cleaned for you. You just tell the Chinaman to send the bill to my office." The man had friendly crinkles around his face, and his washed-out blue eyes twinkled with intelligence. He was all dressed up with a long, black bow tie, clean, black suit, and shined-up shoes.

"Now don't you worry about these old, dusty trail clothes, mister. They got worse on 'em than a little whiskey," Slocum said easily. "In fact, the whiskey's probably good for 'em." He downed his beer and turning to the bartender, yelled for two drinks, motioning to both glasses.

The old gent wouldn't let him pay. "I insist," he said firmly. "These're on me. The least a clumsy man can do."

"I thank you, sir." Slocum took a heavy swallow and said, "In town for the Nakes wedding?"

"Nope. Well, yes. I come in for the wedding, but I don't really know them boys that well except to say hello to." He took a delicate sip of his drink and smacked his lips. "I really come in to have a few and be sociable and to play a game of chess with my friend Goldstein—he puts out the paper. Damn tough player he is too. By the way . . ." He thrust out his right hand. "Name's Stark. G. Tobin Stark. You have that bill sent to me now. Call me G.T. Everybody does."

"Pleased. John Slocum."

Both men were leaning up against the bar, sipping at their drinks. G.T. sighed and said, "Good stuff, this. I'll tell you, don't get as much of a chance to come around since I started up the new business—I'm in hauling freight. Just started up a couple of months ago." He looked over at Slocum. "You in for the wedding, Mr. Slocum? Don't look much like a miner."

"Call me John. No, sir. Just passin' through and saw the bright lights. Thought I'd do a little socializing myself." Slocum didn't want to ask about Tudor yet. For just a little while, even in this small way, he wanted to be involved with the little everyday things of life. It gave him pleasure to live like normal people lived, even though he knew he never did live anything like a normal life. He spent so much time running from something, or after something else, that he felt he had to have a little rest from it. There was plenty of time.

Slocum had passed many houses and many lives in his travels. He had always been after something, and he had always wondered what the people he saw did with their time. How did they pass the days and nights? Usually he only saw them in passing, or in trouble, or got a glimpse of them in a lighted window. Now he wanted to find out more about the man he was with.

"Say you've started up a business? Haulin', you said?"

That started G.T. off.

Slocum learned a lot about G.T.'s business, but he could see why Gerry was always so interested in people's stories—you found out a great deal by listening. In the couple of hours he spent talking and drinking with Stark, Slocum learned that hauling freight was a lot like running cattle; you had to worry about a million little details (and always missed a few), you had to work your ass off from early until late, you were at the mercy of the elements, and you spent a lot of time going from one place to another with too much time to think.

The two men joked and talked, sharing the warmth of liquor and conversation. They watched the people around them, and talked about them for a while. Slocum found that he enjoyed G.T.'s company—he seemed a hardworking and practical man. Slocum especially liked his dry sense of humor—G.T. called himself an independent from Independence, Missouri.

"Funny thing," G.T. said after a while. "I do enjoy your company, young man." Slocum raised his glass in thanks. "And *I* enjoy being referred to as a young man."

"But we are very different people, I can see that," G.T. went on. Slocum nodded in agreement. "You see . . ." G.T. had to raise his voice; the bar had gotten rowdier as the hours went on. "I like to build and make a strong nest. You, you sound like the type who's always searchin' something out. Bet you don't know what it is half the time either."

"You're right about that. Except this time, I do know what I'm searching for. I'm fixin' to look up someone who's supposed to live around here, name of Hal Tudor."

"Hal Tudor! Holy shit, you're a friend of Tudor and that bunch?" G.T. looked surprised and more than a little unhappy. "John Slocum, I may have misjudged, but you don't look like you belong with that crowd."

"Well, for starters, I'm not a friend of Tudor's— I don't even know him—I'm just bringing him a message from somebody he used to scout with. I was just told he was around here."

G.T. smiled again, and put his hand over his heart. "I got to tell you, I'm right nervous around anyone who says he's a friend of that one. There's no deviltry that hasn't been blamed on him and that bunch—and with good reason too. Why, the sight of that Tudor alone is enough to send a body to the

nearest church. I'm tellin' you, boy, forget that
message; stay away from them."

Slocum smiled. He remembered his thoughts on
the Plank Road when he'd first glimpsed Milford
Mountain rising through the desert heat. "Thanks,
G.T., but I kinda promised. I've already been
plenty warned about Tudor. Whereabouts you think
I can find him?"

"That I don't rightly know. Got to be nearby,
though. The four of 'em come altogether sometimes over to the general store." He shook his head.
"Bunch like that . . . people generally steer clear.
Even the law manages to be somewheres else when
they come around. I tell you, if only a few of the
stories they tell are true. . . ."

"There are four of them now?"

Stark looked at John for a while without saying
anything. "I'm not gonna ask you any questions,
son. But one of these days, I'd like for you to tell
me the whole story—that a deal? It'll give me
something to look forward to."

"It's a deal." Slocum looked away, smiling, still
sipping his beer.

"Be a whopper of a tale, I'll bet. Anyway. Yeah,
there's four. Tudor you seem to know about already. Be wary of him. Two are twin brothers—
mean as hell and tough. One's named Mil, the other
goes by Dan. Dan's always showin' off his knife-
throwin'; he was supposed to have been in a carny-
val or somethin' a few years back. Them two are
big, but plenty stupid, it seems to me. They do what
Tudor tells 'em to—won't squat without he says
so. But I'll tell you, I can see why. Gunman by the

name of Deweese is the fourth one. Fancies himself
a wizard with a six-gun—and he is real fast. Always braggin' on the men he's shot down. A small,
nervous man, he is. Outside of Tudor, I'd say he's
the toughest one of the bunch. Something terrible
in those eyes. Easy to recognize—always the
smallest man in the crowd. Always tries to dress
real sharp too . . . good Southron manners, but easy
to rile. Looks respectable, but he's as crazy a loon
as the rest of 'em. You might get a chance to see
him for yourself soon enough. I just saw him in
here a little while ago."

"Sounds like a tough bunch."

"That they are. Like I say, even the law steers
clear."

"What about the mine owners? They can hire a
lot of firepower, or bring in the kind of law that
won't be afraid to hunt them down. They let Tudor
do whatever he pleases?"

The old man looked for a spittoon, hawked, and
let fly. "Mine owners don't give a shit. So long as
Tudor stays away from the mine and the payroll,
and don't try to organize the miners into a union
or some such, they won't spend time worrying
about him. No, that one's too smart to get into a
war with the mines, I'll tell you that. Though, if
anybody could give them a dance it'd be him."

Slocum and G.T. finished their drinks in silence.
Slocum seemed lost in thought. G.T. watched him,
wondering what he could possibly be up to. I'll tell
you, whatever it is, it's dangerous enough to be
worth another drink, G.T. thought. He ordered another round.

When Slocum was handed the glass, he said, "Know anything about Milford Mountain?"

"Milford, eh?" G.T. said. "You seen it?"

Slocum nodded. "Just caught a look from the road."

G.T. went on. "Only one way to get to the top. You think they're up there? No. Don't answer that. Straight from the Plank Road—that road you come to town on?—there's a trail that runs up to the top. If they're up there, they'll see you comin' for a long time." G.T. held his glass up to toast Slocum. *"Moritori."*

"Whatever you said," Slocum answered, toasting back. Both drained their glasses.

Stark asked, "When you plannin' on deliverin' this, uh, message?"

Slocum looked into the empty glass, tilting the slight residue this way and that. "Well, I figured to get going before the sun comes up . . . I'll need a good night's rest . . . so I should be gettin' on about now."

"You got a place to stay?"

"No, I don't. I thought to sleep out. It's a mite cold, but I never minded sleeping under the stars." Slocum smiled at his new friend. "Hope we run into each other again sometime."

Stark smiled back, "I do too, I'll tell you. We'll have some yarns to swap . . . though I bet yours'll be more exciting." As the two shook hands, he said, "Godspeed."

Slocum nodded, and walked away through the raucous crowd into the night.

Just as he'd taken the reins and was about to

mount up, Slocum saw a small, neatly dressed man walk out of the same saloon alone. Strange, he hadn't noticed him. Slocum looked him up and down—small as a child; no more than five feet tall. As the little man came through the bat-wing doors, carefully fitting a new bowler hat on his head, he looked right and left, quickly scanned the windows and roofs across the street, and glanced behind him. Slocum could see that his own presence had been registered immediately. *This must be Deweese.* The gunman looked back and saw that Slocum was still studying him.

John was quite engrossed in his examination of the man not ten feet from where he stood. Deweese certainly was an interesting character, and truly stood out. He didn't look the type to join with the likes of Tudor, though. The man's shirt was clean and buttoned all the way to the top button. Because he was so small, oversized pants were stuffed into surprisingly neat ankle-high boots with low heels. The pants looked to be a good, soft material and were also quite clean. His prominent paunch made him look like a successful, but unhappy, banker.

He don't look very impressive. Except for one thing—his weapon. John hadn't seen many of the heavy Le Mat revolvers—they had a second cylinder that could be turned up to fire buckshot—since the war. Most gunmen thought them too clumsy, and Slocum would have thought that a man with hands as small as Deweese's would have had a hard time with its bulk. Still, it was a reliable and deadly weapon—J. E. B. Stuart had sworn by his. It should have looked ridiculous sitting there tight and high against the man's waist; gun and holster very nearly covered him from hip to knee. But it actually had the effect of making Deweese look bigger.

How can he walk with that thing banging up against his leg? Slocum thought idly.

"Might I help you, suh?"

Slocum looked into his face. Unlike Stark, John didn't see anything special in his pale eyes. Maybe he'd seen too many pairs of cold, hard eyes in his time. While the horse was between them, John undid the thong over the hammer of his side arm.

Walking out from behind the horse, he politely said, "Excuse me?"

"I ahst you, suh, if ah maht help you." The little man's slow drawl was soft. Virginia, John thought. Unmistakable.

"Help me?"

"Yes. You seem to be studyin' me rather closely."

There was no anger in Deweese's voice—there was no emotion of any kind, in fact. John realized what probably made the man in front of him so dangerous. He never gave any kind of warning before he struck. Suddenly, Slocum's sense of danger was very strong. He was going to have to be very careful.

"I'm sorry. I haven't seen too many Le Mats since the war."

"Deweese studied him calmly for a moment before answering. "Is that so? And on what side were you engaged during that glorious conflict? If I might inquire?"

"The South."

"Ah, and so was I. But the War Between the States has been over these many years. And though we were perhaps comrades in arms at that time, suh, I must say that I do not enjoy bein' the object of your close scrutiny." He paused, and then continued in that same polite way. "In fact, I object to it. Do I make myself clear?"

Touchy bastard. Well, now, this can go two ways. Either I fight him now, or let it go and fight him later.

"Your name Deweese?"

"Yes, suh, it is. Might I have your name?" Without taking his eyes off John, Deweese rested both hands on his belt; in easy reaching distance of his weapon.

"Slocum. John Slocum."

"Well. Mistuh Slocum. Seems to me I've heard your name a time or two. If I remember correctly, you're a gunman of some repute. Like myself. And why is it that you've come to see me?"

"Haven't come to see you, Deweese. It's Hal Tudor I've come to see. Have a message for him from an old friend."

"And what makes you think I can help you?"

"I don't. We just happen to have struck up a conversation. I guess you're the one asking all the questions. I only asked you your name."

"Mistuh Slocum. Like myself, Mistuh Tudor likes his privacy and freedom. Perhaps it would be best if you told me the message and I brought it for you. Then you could ride off and be about your own business."

"Sorry. I promised I'd give the message directly to him. Why don't I just ride back to Milford Mountain with you?"

Deweese pursed his lips in annoyance. "Could you do me the courtesy of telling how you knew that Mistuh Tudor was residing there?"

"His friend said that's where he might be. I—"

"Who is this . . . friend . . . you keep mentioning, suh?"

No one had come in or out of the saloon; no one had walked anywhere near them since they had first met. The two men, one large and muscular, the other soft and small, were free to focus all their considerable attentions upon each other.

"You ask a damn lot of questions, you know that?"

Deweese's eyes narrowed. "Do I now?" he asked in that same calm unhurried tone. "Does that bother you, suh?"

"Look Deweese. I'm not trying to start a fight with you."

"It seems to me that you are trying to provoke me. I won't have it. If you persist in being an annoyance, I shall have to deal with you."

Slocum was getting tired of the man's manner. He managed to be polite and insulting at the same time. Besides, Slocum knew he'd aroused Deweese's suspicions; if he let him get back to Tudor and the others, John wouldn't stand a chance . . . even if he did finally think of a plan. No. John could see where this was all heading. It was time to lower the odds.

Without thinking about what he was doing, Slocum said, "Then we'll say good-bye." Reaching up with his left hand, he seemed to tug his hat brim lower and turn to his right and walk away. Suddenly John spun his hat at Deweese's face. At the same time he fell to his right, quickly pulling the Colt across his body, thumb pulling the hammer back, forefinger pressing the trigger. He snapped his arm out before him, concentrating an instant on his aim, and released the hammer.

Deweese *was* fast. John had to give him that. The huge Le Mat was clearing the holster while Deweese instinctively ducked Slocum's hat. Both men fired at about the same time, though Slocum's shot was first by a fraction of a second. Deweese's slug tore through the empty air where Slocum had stood before falling. Slocum's bullet hit Deweese just to the left of his chest's center, propelling him back through the saloon's bat-wing doors. Before those doors slammed shut, two more bullets followed Deweese, hitting him just over the stomach, slapping him back a further step. As he fell, blood spraying from the impact of the heavy shells, Deweese fired twice—both shots went wild, into the floor planks on his right. As he lay twitching on the floor, a final shot from his gun ricocheted off the doorjamb.

John picked himself up from the ground, dusted himself off, and walked into the now-silent saloon. He stooped to pick up his hat on the way. The only sounds that could be heard were yells and shouts from the street behind him. They sounded miles away. In the bar, all were frozen, watching as Slocum gingerly used his boot to move the Le Mat away from Deweese's hand. Slocum holstered the Colt but left the thumb-guard off, watching the crowd.

The air was so still, the dust that the dead man's body stirred up still hung in the air over him, shining in the lights.

G.T. was the first to move, and everyone started to talk at once. No one came over to him, however, except Stark. "John you are a *year's* worth of entertainment."

"He forced it, G.T."

"I don't think anyone will doubt that. He's been starting fights over imagined insults for nearly a year now. I tell you, John, town'll probably award you a medal; sheriff'll probably ask you to be deputy."

"You think he's got any friends that'll try to ambush me?"

"Not damn likely, boy. I tell you, he only came to town for a woman, a drink, and a fight. Always kept to himself—'cept when he was with Tudor and his bunch." G.T. stopped and motioned John to turn around. Pointing out a tall, distinguished man, sporting several turquoise rings and a turquoise string tie, who was supervising the removal of the body, he said, "Sheriff Sidman."

John walked over to him and began to explain what had happened. The sheriff hooked his thumbs under his lapels and listened politely. Around them several men worked at taking Deweese's body away. After waiting for John to finish, Sidman asked, "You interested in a deputy job, Mister Slocum?"

John turned to smile at G.T. and said, "No, thank you. I'm not."

About twenty minutes later, after saying a second good-bye to Stark, Slocum left town.

He slept well that night. He dreamed no dream.

He was riding back toward Milford Mountain before the sun came up.

All the way back, during the long day's ride in the rising heat, his mind was a blank. He'd had a good night's rest—slept like a baby, in fact. Woke easily, felt good. His brain was just turned in on itself, it seemed. Like it was working hard on a problem, and didn't have room for anything else.

After midday, near the place where he'd first spotted the mountain, Slocum stopped and said with wonder in his voice, "I'll be damned!"

It had come to him all at once. Without actually thinking about it, he'd been trying to get at what it was the wolves had told him about Tudor. A few times, it had seemed like it was on the tip of his tongue, but the answer had slipped back, unreachable. Slocum hadn't worried on it; he was prepared to wait until it did come. He'd had that much faith that it *would* come to him.

And it did.

It surely did.

How *could* it have taken so long. Of course . . . the wolves . . . a message for Tudor from a friend . . .

Slocum felt a whole range of emotions—from elation to fear, and amazement. He was elated because the time was here, there was no more waiting, because the search was shorter and easier than he could have hoped for. There was fear, of course; there was more than a good chance that this little trip would mean his death—and maybe not an easy one at that. Finally, John was amazed—mystified was more like it—by the whole business . . . ghosts and dreams and messages from beyond the grave; it was more than a man wanted to puzzle out.

For the hundredth time, he wondered what Gerry would make of it all. John Slocum had given up trying.

I'll just be fucking damned.

Life was just too puzzling; it was such an awful mix-up that a man couldn't go through it without cursing.

From this distance, the mountain looked like a tree stump, sitting alone on the desert floor. There was a range of hills and peaks to the west and the east, but they were some distance away. G.T. was right: Whoever rode toward the mountain would be visible for a long time. There was virtually no way to come up on the place unnoticed. Tudor, if he *was* there, had picked a good place to hide. From here also, the sides of the peak looked sheer, and scored, like some gigantic creature had raked claws down its sides. There had to be other trails up to its flat top, but they were bound to be steep, narrow, and easily defended. John only knew of the one. Tudor had picked his lair very well.

Slocum decided to waste as little time as possible. He checked his weapons; made sure that the knife was secure in the top of his boot, put the extra revolver in his saddlebag. He was pretty sure that they'd take away his rifle and gun belt. If his plan worked, he'd be able to get to the hidden pistol and the knife. It was the only way he could think of to do the job and still walk out in one piece.

The whole plan depended on Tudor letting him into the camp. It could only work if Tudor was as crazy as John thought he was; it could only work if they decided not to shoot him right away. It could only work if Tudor himself was there and not off someplace else.

It was a slim, slim chance.

When he had done all he could do, he sat down and thought it through one more time—just like it was a chess game . . . *if I do this and he does that, then I do that.* . . . When he was sure, he rode straight for Milford Mountain.

Mil saw the lone rider coming across from the Plank Road and wondered who the hell could be so crazy. Whoever that fool was, he had to be heading up this way. There wasn't any place he *could* be going except up here. He hoped Tudor would let him play with this one awhile before they killed him. It had been too long since he'd had any fun. *Dan got the last one and killed him right off, just about. What a waste.*

Better let him know that we've got a visitor coming. Tudor had both brothers jumping through hoops—because he got them the kind of entertainment they craved, and because they were both terrified of him. There was no telling what he would do, so both tried to keep from angering him—although they both enjoyed seeing Tudor get angry at someone else.

Mil made his way through the ruined, roofless buildings and pits. He always wondered what was down in these holes in the ground. *Probably buried gold—why else dig all them holes on top of a mountain in the middle of nowhere?* Tudor would never let them explore, however. Told them both to never, never go near the pits . . . said his Wolf had warned him that spirits lived in the darkness under their feet . . . if you went into the pits it would let them spirits out. *Shit, that Wolf business makes me nervous as hell. It's crazy stuff.* But he'd never dare tell Tudor that.

Picking his way and maneuvering his bulk carefully, he found Tudor propped up against a stone wall. At first, he thought the man was sleeping through the day's awful heat; his eyes were closed and he was breathing lightly. You never knew with him, though; you had to be very careful.

Brother Dan was cleaning his rifle not too far away. When he saw Mil had left his post, he figured that something was up. At least he hoped it was something important—he didn't want Tudor losing his temper and, God forbid, calling up the Wolf. It was terrible when he did that. *Hope we get to have a little fun.*

As Mil approached, the big man's eyes suddenly opened. "Someone's coming," Tudor said. It wasn't a question.

Shit! I hate when he does that. If he knows, then why'n hell do we have to keep watch all the time?

Mil stopped. "Yeah. One rider. What do you want to do?"

Tudor smiled. "What do *you* want to do? Seems like it's your turn."

The fat man's hand slipped to his crotch. "Oh, boy," he said. "Let's have some fun."

Slocum made his way on the narrow, torturous trail winding up the mountain's face. At any moment he expected to hear a shot and feel the impact of a bullet, or to look up and see a boulder rolled down, about to sweep him from the trail. Right now, he was wondering how he could have been so sure he'd be allowed to come up to the top without being killed.

If they let me up, Rick, we'll have a chance.

He wasn't so sure now that they'd give him that chance. Slocum hoped they were curious enough to find out why he'd come. There was no question in his mind that they were there, watching and waiting. If he was allowed up, it still didn't promise to be easy. There was no guarantee that he'd be able to fool the three gunmen or that he'd be fast enough to bring down all three before one of them put a bullet or a knife into him.

One thing at a time. Let's just get up there first.

Up there, he'd have to be calm, he'd have to take control of the situation quickly. If he didn't, he would be lost. Tudor and his henchmen would make short work of him . . . or worse, they would make his death long and hard. Slocum knew he wouldn't have a lot of time. He would have to confuse Tudor. If he could do that he'd have more than half the battle won. If he could keep them off balance, only for a little while, he'd be able to get to his weapons. Then he would have a fighting chance. That was all he was asking for—a chance to fight.

Coming up the last leg of the trail, Slocum tried to put all that away. The time for thinking and planning was past.

11

Slocum had just gotten to the flat top of Milford Mountain when he saw Hal Tudor not ten feet in front of him. He reined up. He didn't see the two brothers.

Tudor stood straight in the burning sunlight, still wearing the tight, stained clothes he'd been wearing in the dream at the Whites' cabin. His hair and beard were just as greasy and unkempt as they had been then.

But he looked twice as big and three times as mean.

He was leaning on a rifle, smiling a death's-head grin. Directing that awful grin up at Slocum, he said, "C'mon in. Set a spell."

Getting down slowly, Slocum started to walk toward the barefoot giant. He was about to open his mouth and start what he'd planned, when suddenly he was struck from behind with something heavy and hard. He landed on his face in the dirt. His head was filled with pain; it felt twice its normal size. He had trouble focusing his eyes; everything was blurry and shifting.

As he tried to stand, Slocum's legs slipped out from under him; he seemed to have lost control, unable to get his body to move the way he wanted it to. He heard a high-pitched voice whine, "You hit him too hard, damn it! I don't want to fuck a dead man."

Slocum was roughly grabbed and searched by two pairs of hands. When his gun belt was taken away, one of those pairs of hands squeezed his genitals hard. Slocum heard the high-pitched giggle when he couldn't suppress a yelp of pain. The voice spoke up again. "Hey, just like a pig."

Slocum was in a panic now. It had gone too fast for him—he wasn't going to have any time. He couldn't get enough coordination to even begin to struggle. He couldn't even get his voice to work.

Carried the few feet to where Tudor continued to stand, Slocum was flung to the ground. Surprisingly, when his head bounced off a rock on the way down, his vision began to clear a little bit. *That knocked some sense into me. Good thing I hit my head.* He shook like a hound coming out of the water and rolled over onto his back. Just as everything came into focus and John began to get control over his limbs, Tudor took a step over and placed one foot on top of Slocum's face, pressing down.

For the first few moments, Slocum had to fight hard not to vomit. Tudor's foot smelled as bad as it looked—like spoiled fetid cheese. He could hardly breathe—the foul thing almost covered his whole face, it was so large. The feel of the huge foot was horrible, hard like a huge scab, crusted and filthy. He could hear the other two guffawing off to one side.

He recognized Tudor's voice asking with deceptive politeness, "What are you doing up here, son?"

Slocum tried to speak, but his voice was muffled. He knew that if he opened his mouth too wide, he *would* throw up. He tried to move the foot, but couldn't budge it. It was impossible to move Tudor's foot, no matter how hard he tried, and he couldn't move his head to either side. Suddenly, John felt a rifle barrel poked into his balls. Tudor pressed harder, and he heard the raspy voice say, "Aw, hell, who cares? Let's blow his balls off."

Slocum tried to yell, but all he could manage was a bleat. *I've lost!*

He was sure it would be his last thought.

"No! You promised!"

"Okay, okay. Damn your eyes."

John felt the foot lift, then press down even harder. He heard Tudor's voice, calm and ominous. "Don't try to lie to this old beaver now, or I'll let Danny boy over there skin you alive."

Again, Slocum heard the whining voice. "But you promised him to *me*!"

Tudor shouted, "*After* you've had him, damn it!"

The scaly weight was finally lifted and Slocum quickly rolled over, spitting and wiping his mouth with his gritty sleeve. Looking up, he saw Tudor staring at him hard. He was flanked by two men—*Mil and Dan*—who would have seemed large if they hadn't been standing next to Hal Tudor. Slocum quickly registered filthy clothes, unshaven faces, and the obese bulk of the two identical forms. One of them was holding Slocum's rifle.

"While this child here is tellin' his tale, Dan, why don't you search his rig."

"Okay, Hal," said the man in a surprisingly deep voice.

The one with the high voice must be Mil, Slocum thought. I've got to make my move now, or they'll find the .45.

Dan began to walk toward Slocum's horse.

Slocum got to his knees, threw back his head, and put everything he had into one long, mad howl. *That feels good.*

It seemed to John, looking out of the corner of his eye, that Tudor jumped back ten feet.

Dan stopped dead in his tracks and wailed, "Oh, sweet Jesus, not another one!"

Slocum jumped to his feet and continued to howl for all he was worth. Both Mil and Dan backed up clumsily, while Tudor stood, mouth agape. Laughing and howling, Slocum moved his head from side to side, herding the three together. The two brothers got behind Tudor, seemingly for protection, though their boss was so surprised he couldn't seem to move a muscle. Slocum's horse had shifted, made nervous by all the commotion, off to their left.

Slocum was beginning to feel good now—he'd gotten their attention and shifted them off balance. He wasn't going to let them have a chance to regain their wits.

Abruptly breaking off his howling, Slocum said in a loud, stentorian voice, "Hal Tudor! Wolf told me all about you!"

There's the bait.

If he looked surprised before, Tudor was completely poleaxed now. He dropped his rifle and stuck his head forward, eyes popping. "Wolf? You talk to *my* Wolf?" he whispered.

Slocum could actually hear fear in his voice.

With the biggest shit-eating grin he could manage without busting his face, Slocum said cheerily, "Sure do. Told me to come right on up here and warn you." Slocum tilted his head and winked broadly. "He *always* knows what to do."

Tudor leaned forward, eyes blinking and features contorting. He hadn't closed his mouth since John had mentioned Wolf. The two brothers hadn't said a word or taken their eyes off Slocum. They stood still as statues.

"What . . . what did he say?" Tudor couldn't stop from stammering. "What did he . . . he want to warn me . . . about?"

Now the hook.

Slocum looked around cautiously and motioned Tudor to come closer.

Tudor leaned so far forward that he nearly fell over.

In a low whisper, Slocum said, "Rick White is coming."

Tudor let out a bloodcurdling scream. Both brothers yelped; it seemed to Slocum that they jumped five feet straight up. Slocum turned away and started to walk toward his horse.

"Wait! What else did Wolf say? What does he want me to do?"

Hooked.

Slocum walked behind his horse. "He says you should use magic against him."

"Magic?"

"A magic bullet," Slocum said, pulling out the .45. He shot Tudor first.

The bullet took Tudor square in the chest, knocking the big man back a step. He stood with his arms away from his sides, dumbly watching the spreading black stain.

Slocum, still standing behind the horse, the gun held straight out, fired calmly at Mil and then Dan. Neither had a chance to react. Mil's head burst into a red flower. Dan was hit in the neck, his head flopping over sideways comically as muscle and blood sprayed. Both hit the ground and didn't move.

Tudor whispered, "Magic." Then he slowly bent, trying to pick up his rifle. John walked around the horse, not hurrying, and shot him twice; once in the shoulder, knocking his arm away from the weapon, and then in the knee. The second shot toppled Tudor off his feet and spun him onto his back more than an arm's length from his rifle.

Slocum smiled and said, "I lied. *Rick* sent me."

As Slocum walked to within a few feet of the bleeding man, Tudor begun to yell, "Wolf! Wolf!" He glared at Slocum and howled, reaching for the rifle.

Slocum raised his pistol. "Not this time." The bullet punched into Tudor's heart and he fell back into the dust, still as death itself.

Reloading and holstering his weapon, Slocum turned the cooling body onto its stomach and pulled the knife from his boot. He grabbed a full hand of Tudor's hair in his left hand and pulled up hard until the head came up from the ground. Trying not to think about what he was doing, or about the slimy feel of Tudor's filthy hair, John cut deeply across the forhead just below the hairline and through the hair around to the back of the head. Then he let go. He wiped the blade on Tudor's back, leaving a trail of hair and blood, and returned the knife to his boot. He straddled the body and sat on the lower part of the dead man's back, then gathered up the long, dirty locks in both hands and put his right foot up between Tudor's shoulders.

John leaned back and pulled hard, pushing his foot forward. The scalp ripped slowly along the cut and popped off. Tudor's face fell heavily, back into the dust.

Holding the bloody trophy away from him as far as he could, Slocum waved it until the blood stopped spraying from it. He knew what he had to do. He didn't think about how he knew. He just knew.

It was a short walk over to the cliff. By the time he reached it, Slocum noticed buzzards approaching. *How do they know so quickly?* He held the scalp out over the cliff, and three owls appeared from below as if they'd been waiting for this very moment. They flew up quickly; one of them grabbed the scalp, tugged it from John's hand, and they all flew off.

Slocum watched until he could no longer make them out against the mountains and the sky.

It's done.

12

It was morning when John Slocum rode into Golden heading straight for the saloon where Gerry worked. He hoped his friend would be tending bar this early. He'd been looking forward to this conversation for quite a while—especially on the long trip back—savoring it in his mind.

He hitched the horse and walked quickly into the room. The smells of liquor and smoke hung in the air. There were no customers. A thin, balding man wearing an apron was sitting on the bar.

Must be the day bartender.

The man looked up from the newspaper he was reading. As Slocum walked up, the man folded it, lifted his feet up, and swung his legs around. He jumped down behind the bar with a hollow thump.

"Morning. What can I do for you?"

"Morning," Slocum replied. "What time does Gerry get here?"

The bartender looked at Slocum. "Gerry?"

"You know. The muscular, white-haired gent

who tends bar here at night? Everybody knows Gerry."

The man looked away. "Oh. Him." He didn't sound happy. "A couple of people have asked about him. You a friend?"

"Yeah. Where is he?"

"I'm sorry, mister. He killed himself about a month ago. Went in the back room after closing one night and just blew his own brains out."

Slocum stared at the man for a long time, his mind a blank. Finally, he said, knowing how stupid it must sound, "You're joking."

"No, mister. I ain't."

"But he was the sanest, smartest, strongest man I ever met. How . . . But why?" Slocum couldn't seem to put the right words together.

"I never knew the man. You could go down to the sheriff's office; they probably know more about it."

Slocum slumped and turned away. "No. It doesn't matter."

Turning back to the barman after a few steps, Slocum said, "What kind of world *is* this?"

The bartender had returned to the paper. "I'm sure I don't know, mister," he said without looking up.

Riding out of town, Slocum struggled to understand. It couldn't be true; it just couldn't be true.

Slocum turned east, into the sun, riding slow. Rolling and firing cigarette after cigarette, he rode, thinking hard. *What do I do now. Where do I go?* He thought for a minute, and headed for Coty.

•   •   •

It was a bright day when Slocum rode into Coty. He interrupted a boy's whistling at the livery stable and found out where Stark's office was. Walking down the bright street, John moved through crowds of miners to the opposite end of the little town. He saw a tiny, ramshackle office with a sign that read, "G. Tobin Stark Hauling," backed up by a yard with three heavy wagons. Horses were visible in a stable at the rear of the yard. All sorts of harness and equipment lay around, and several men were working on some kind of repairs on a fourth wagon set up in front of the office. Walking past the men, he rapped on the closed door.

"Enter!" Stark's voice shouted from inside. Slocum pulled the door open, looked around quickly, and said, "That's a pretty high-toned greeting for such a small place." The office was only big enough to hold the desk, covered with stacks of paper, two boxes filled with papers on the floor, and the chair Stark was sitting in; there was just room enough for Stark to get out from behind the desk. John wasn't sure if he could fit himself in if he closed the door. He left it open, even though the workmen made it difficult to hear.

Stark leaned out over his desk as far as he could and thrust out his hand. "Why, John, you temerarious old scalawag! I didn't expect to see you so soon. How 'n hell are you?"

Slocum took the hand firmly. "I need your advice. Whyn't I let you buy me breakfast or a drink?"

"Everything all right, John?" Stark said quietly. "You in need of help?"

"No, no, nothing like that. I just need the benefit of some of that hard-earned wisdom of yours." He smiled and tugged at Stark's hand, which was still shaking his.

"Well, hell, yes, boy. Breakfast sounds just about right." He shouted to no one in particular, "Goin' t' lunch!" Then he squeezed around the desk, chuckling. "Bound to be out of the ordinary, knowin' you."

In the crowded, bustling cafe, surrounded by crowds of workingmen shouting and eating, Slocum told Stark the whole story. He began with Cahill and ended with Gerry's suicide. He left nothing out. He hardly touched his food.

Stark, who'd wasted no time while listening closely, pushed back his empty plate, sipped his coffee, and shook his head. "Damn. What a tale. Never heard the like. Never would have *imagined* the like. Why, no one could make up such a whopper as that."

He sat silently for a few minutes, staring into his black coffee. Finally, he looked up and said, "I'll tell you this—you're alive and Gerry is dead. I guess you know how to survive better 'n him. Seems to me that what you did was right and you come through it alive. That counts for a lot in my book, I'll tell you."

John looked around the busy room, at the waitresses and cooks, at the men walking in and out. Without looking at his friend, he said, "Thanks for that. Yeah, I'm alive, but what now? What if I just backslide and start feelin' sorry for myself again?"

Stark cocked his head and closed one eye. "That's up to you, son," he said seriously. "Maybe you shouldn't be worried so much about what's in the past. You should be thinkin' hard about how to fix what you don't like about today—and don't tell me it can't be fixed." He pointed a bony finger in John's face. "Everything can be fixed if you're willin' to pay the price and do the work. You have to have a little faith in your abilities . . . and they are *con*siderble, I'll tell you."

John looked around some more, thinking. At last he said, "You got a little money you can lend me?"

Without hesitating, Stark said, "Sure. How much you need?"

John smiled. "Oh, not much. I have to go see a little lady name of Moira in a saloon."

Stark smiled right back. "Good place to start."